# The Date Gallery

Dr. Sharon Campbell-Phillips

pencil

ISBN 978-93-5610-829-5
© Dr. Sharon Campbell-Phillips 2022
Published in India 2022 by Pencil

*A brand of*
One Point Six Technologies Pvt. Ltd.
123, Building J2, Shram Seva Premises,
Wadala Truck Terminal, Wadala (E)
Mumbai 400037, Maharashtra, INDIA
**E** connect@thepencilapp.com
**W** www.thepencilapp.com



DISCLAIMER: *This is a work of fiction. Names, characters, places, events and incidents are the products of the author's imagination. The opinions expressed in this book do not seek to reflect the views of the Publisher.*

# Author biography

My name is Dr. Sharon Campbell-Phillips. I am from Trinidad and Tobago. I am very enthusiastic about community work and the development of others. I am also very passionate about conducting research and writing as it allows me the opportunity to share my knowledge with others and educate them as well as enhance and develop myself.

I am currently employed with the local government of Trinidad and Tobago where I work in the Division of Community Development. This Division is dedicated to developing communities so that persons' standard of living can be enhanced.

My writing career began when I was approached by a classmate from Bangladesh to collaborate and write professionally. I accepted the challenge and we began writing together. When I received my first publication, I was very excited and was motivated to continue writing, I am also a Doctor of Health Sciences. My passion for writing allows me to complete individual projects, as well as collaborate with others to produce impressive work.

Phone: +1868 7511022
Email: sharoncampbell433@gmail.com

# CONTENTS


CHAPTER ONE.................................................... 7

CHAPTER TWO ................................................. 20

CHAPTER THREE .............................................. 32

CHAPTER FOUR ............................................... 46

CHAPTER FIVE ................................................. 59

CHAPTER SIX..................................................... 72

CHAPTER SEVEN .............................................. 82

CHAPTER EIGHT ............................................... 92

# Preface

Having just celebrated their first wedding anniversary, Charly and T.G., as she had found out to name him, were tremendously happy. Because of the hours that they had spent reviewing their dreams, they had ended up really close before the conference, and the transition to living together had been smooth for them. Giving up her cherished bungalow and the dream of proudly owning it at some point have been clean, and she had adapted nicely to sharing T. G.'s domestic with him."Hi, Sleepy Head."As Charly got here slowly unsleeping, hair messed up and cheeks flushed with sleep, she became conscious that T.G. Became mendacity there looking at her. He told her regularly how lovely she changed into, and what kind of he loved her, so she never had reason to doubt his feelings. A broad smile lit up her face as she got here absolutely conscious."Oh my gosh, T.G., do you have any twins in your circle of relatives?" "None that I recognize of. Why?"Well if the dream I just had is any indication, that's approximately to alternate. In the dream, you and I were every preserving a tiny toddler - one boy and one woman. How cool is that?"Is this dream for actual?" T. G. Was with a bit of luck curious."Because it changed into an early morning dream, it could clearly be about communication we are going to have these days, or it may be approximately a few elements  of work because toddlers can represent new thoughts, or it is able to imply simply what it says - we are going to have twins.''Well, come here, my love, and let's make it appear." Pulling her into his arms, T. G. Went right away approximately the business of planting the seeds that might produce the crop he hoped to create. Charly, along with her regular enthusiasm, gave him all of her help, alongside all of her love and adoration. Meanwhile, little souls chuckled with glee as they hovered around them, knowing that they'd made a super desire for their destiny mother and father-to-be.

# CHAPTER ONE

What the hell, Charly nodded, I've already misplaced the task so there's nothing to be received by being polite."Very nicely, Mr. McKinnon. But I'd like to make a small bet with you. If I win, you rent me. If I lose, you rent any man you want."As she become speaking, Charly noticed the muscle in his jaw relax, the hostility in his eyes alternate to interest and speculation."And the character of this guess?" You pick any enterprise documents you wish and provide them to me. I'll carry out the inspections below your supervision. Today is Friday. The guess will start Monday morning at 9:00 and stop at 5:00 p.m. On Wednesday, if you could spare the time, of course. And I'll work without pay. You can make my revenue retroactive while you rent me Thursday. Have we got a deal?"We have a deal, Miss Benson. I'll meet you here at 9:00 on Monday. But don't spend any money yet." And he smiled.It changed into the primary time his face had been comfortable since the interview commenced hours in advance. But the smile wasn't pleasant. It was arrogant, a definite smirk. Oh nicely, she'd gained the primary spherical.Picking up her résumé she stood, stated, "Thank you for your time, gentlemen," and left the room. The tension that have been together with her for the past numerous hours drained away as she shrugged into her coat, under the curious glances of the workplace group of workers.Moving in the direction of the door, she swung around as she heard her call being known. Bearing down on her turned into a nevertheless-boastful Mr. McKinnon, a few documents held loosely in his right hand."You might want to look these over this weekend. We'll do three an afternoon. See you Monday."Taking the documents from him, Charly had time most effective to murmur, "Thank you," earlier than he had grown to become back to the boardroom.Tucking them into her wearing case, alongside her résumé, Charly went out and was given behind the wheel of her SUV. Aware that she became nonetheless below the surveillance of the personnel, she commenced the engine and moved off down the street, out in their line of imaginative and prescient.Why the satan hadn't the manager instructed her that Mr. McKinnon was a showed misogynist? Was it simply her he hated or changed into it-girls in preferred? The manager had confidence that the activity was as accurate as hers two days in the past, after reviewing her qualifications and interviewing her. He'd started the assembly with the Board of Directors was most effective a formality and a courtesy to herself and the administrators.In retrospect, it become clear he'd acknowledged in advance that there'd be a hassle with McKinnon. Suddenly she was struck with the feeling that she'd been set up. Mr. McKinnon had bristled from the instant she had walked in the door and the conflict lines had been firmly drawn. His questions were time and again slanted closer to the problem that her femininity could purpose. Also her size.Was it viable he hadn't been instructed she become a girl? If he'd visible her software and study her call as Charly Benson, he might have assumed she changed into a person. Well, she'd show him!

Five years of intensive study had organized her well for this process and she or he knew she may want to do it, given the hazard. She had spent three years at Mohawk College reading for her Insurance Institute Certificate and had handed inside the top five of her elegance. Then, understanding she'd need an edge due to the fact she changed into trying to break into a person's area, she had spent two more years at Conestoga College in Guelph graduating with an Electrical Technician's papers.So now, she become well certified, maybe even over-certified, and quite aware that Mr. McKinnon's doubts have been nicely founded. Growing up on her dad and mom's dairy farm near Picton, she had recognized the hesitation with which farmers had been accepting women in guys' roles.Girls now were regularly part of alleviation milking groups and were also hired as milk inspectors. She determined it fun that wives and daughters were regularly pressed into providing using tractors with heavy equipment at the back of them, and frequently helped with the milking, feeding, and cleaning around the barns. But just let one among them observe for a job that was historically done via a person and watch the hackles upward push!Leaving the town of Picton at the back, Charly drove, without conscious thought, to her mother and father's retirement home on the outskirts of Belleville. They had sold the farm final year because Charly became the handiest child and had no preference to be a dairy farmer - just a farm Insurance Inspector.So a lot became riding on this activity. She had sold the SUV with a loan from her Dad, had student loans to pay again, and wanted to lease or buy her area so her dad and mom should experience their retirement while not having her underfoot. Monday,

Tuesday, and Wednesday would probably be the three maximum critical days in her lifestyle to date, and she needed to make appropriate.McKinnon's boastful smile possibly intended that he'd selected the maximum difficult documents he ought to find and become in all likelihood looking ahead to her downfall with outstanding glee. To be forewarned become to be forearmed and she or he could be equipped for him. There became nothing she could do about her five-feet-four inches in height, however, she should research and memorize the files till she knew them internal.Telling her mother and father only that she'd been given a three-day trial length, Charly poured over the files until she felt she knew the entirety there has been to know about them. She had observed the only proper away that became inflicting McKinnon to smirk. There became a be aware on it suggesting that the policy should be canceled without delay if upkeep to the barn was not finished. It was dated several weeks in the past. The report additionally informed her there was no mortgage, so the farmer become probable in correct shape financially and his buildings, pigs, and equipment have been nicely insured. So what changed into his hassle? There didn't look like something remarkable about the opposite documents, however, she strongly suspected that they had been also ladies-haters. There could be something to appear out for besides.She checked her virtual camera over cautiously and made certain she had an extra charged battery. Although brokers had been required to put up images with the coverage packages, she knew a few could be missing and others old.As Monday morning approached, she determined herself turning increasingly more frightened.

She had bought a detailed county map and had located the three farms, then deliberate the direction she would comply with to visit them without backtracking.Her next trouble turned into what to wear. She needed to look expert however her garments also had to be washed and worn, so she had offered five serviceable jumpsuits in deep pastel shades. They were sturdy, washable, and pretty attractive with an elasticized waist that emphasized her determination. But she didn't want to put on one on Monday when Mr. McKinnon would be accompanying her. Finally deciding on a couple of chocolate brown trousers and a tan blazer, with a tailor-made old-gold blouse, she braided her waist-duration auburn hair into one long plait which she twined into a knot on the return of her head. Slipping her feet into a snug pair of sand barren region boots, she picked up a matching take hold of the purse, her documents, and digital camera and headed for the car, pulse racing and a knot in her stomach.The power to Picton surpassed in a blur as her mind concentrated on the documents and the statistics she had tried to assimilate. Anything to avoid thinking about Mr. McKinnon and the chance of having him searching over her shoulder each inch of the way. But thoughts of him rushed solidly to the leading edge whilst she pulled up outdoor the workplace at 8:50 to find him already there. All six feet two inches, leaning against his black Cadillac, legs crossed on the ankles, fingers folded across his chest. Determined to hide her nervousness, she drove up beside him and, accomplishing across the width of the automobile, opened the door for him."Good morning, Mr. McKinnon. All set?"Sliding his frame into her little SUV wasn't smooth and he grunted as he attempted to set up his long legs between the sprint and the seat."Sure I'm prepared. I'm just along for the trip. Remember?" He glanced at her, unsmiling, implacable, giving nothing away. Certainly now not pleasant! So it's how it's going to be, she idea, as she pulled far away from the cutback. We'll see. Glancing facet-methods, she realized he hadn't mounted his seatbelt and couldn't withstand telling him to do so."Buckle up, please."Is your riding that bad?" No sarcasm, but no humor changed into evident either."My driving file is super, but why take a chance? Besides, the fines are heavy."As he buckled up, she observed how properly dressed he became, and nearly giggled aloud when she found out they must appear like Mutt and Jeff because his outfit, excluding the shirt, become almost similar to hers. Brown slacks with a knife-sharp crease, tan blazer, and brown loafers, and almost a foot of difference of their heights."Something a laugh you, Miss Benson?"The words were spoken sharply, and Charly found out he would possibly assume she became giggling at him, so determined to come easy. "It just struck me that we'd have the same tailor, judging using our appearances. Will every person believe this wasn't planned?" Frankly, I could not care much less. I'm only involved along with your overall performance, no longer your seems."And that puts me firmly in my location, I wager, God, what a humorless creature! How does his wife stand it?Silence reigned for several miles, and it wasn't till they neared Mr. Baker's farm that he broke it."I expect you're doing Baker's first?"At her nod of agreement, he persevered, "You realize what's required?" Check the kingdom of his barn, more often than not, and tell him he has one week to finish all necessary upkeep, or his coverage might be canceled. Can I ask why it hasn't been completed before now?"Mainly due to the fact we have been without an inspector for some time. But I'm positive you'll manage."Without searching at him, she should again sense the smugness in his solution. But there was also an undercurrent of bitterness in his voice while he cited the previous inspector and she or he wondered in short about it.She became fortunate - very lucky. Because Mr. Baker become simply coming from the barn with a hammer and a fistful of nails as she stepped out of the car. Quickly, she brought herself and Mr. McKinnon and informed him why she become there. It didn't take long to recognize that he turned into normally crotchety and crabby, and failed to like strangers. But she poured on the attraction, praised the efforts he had made in repairing the lacking forums at the barn, and trendy his vintage tractor. When he realized she knew what she became speaking approximately, he started to unbend and walked with her as she made her inspection.While her eyes took in the info about electrical wiring, preferred housekeeping, and the presence of hearth extinguishers, and she or he made short notes on her clipboard, he advised her he'd been inside the health center for an operation, and that his hired man hadn't with protection. She instructed him about her Dad's farm and approximately a puppy pig she'd had once, and all the whilst she changed into aware of Mr. McKinnon simply at the back of them, watching and listening.Out inside the sunshine once more, she seemed across the machine shed and workshop, however, ought to find nothing to criticize."Would you thoughts if I take some pictures for our documents? The ones we have are outdated and have to be renewed."You move ahead and take your images,

Miss Benson. I'll put the kettle on and we'll have a cup of espresso whilst you're finished." He became and walked into the residence.Charly unnoticed McKinnon as she took her pictures, a number of the residence, the barn, and the outbuildings. She turned into conscious that he became once more leaning on the automobile and watching her, however then, that turned into his challenge. When she had completed, she approached the automobile to place the camera in it, however, he was leaning against her door."Excuse me, please. I'd like to eliminate this earlier than I move internally. Coming for a coffee?" "Oh, I wouldn't pass over it for the sector, Miss Benson." He straightened and pulled the door open for her."Keeping you amused, am I?" She realized her query turned into a bit flippant as soon as she uttered it, but his silent watchfulness becomes starting to annoy her."Immensely amused. I have not loved myself this a good deal in years."Small things amuse small minds, she notion, and neglected the sharp appearance he threw her. It became difficult to tell if he turned into being sarcastic, due to the fact his feedback was all added within the identical conversational tone. She decided it become exceptional to mention not anything further, and turned to the house as a substitute. Mr. Baker had set the table with coffee mugs, cream, sugar, serviettes, and a plate of clean desserts. Not looking to offend him, Charly ate one. She became very surprised whilst he admitted he had baked them."Since my wife died, I've learned to do lots of things that I'd by no means completed earlier, like laundry, housecleaning, and cooking. But I experience it."As he became talking, Charly unexpectedly became aware that McKinnon's eyes have been riveted on her left hand wherein curled around her espresso cup. And he becomes frowning. Outside of a murmured "Thank you" to Mr. Baker, he had been silent.Completing a brief excursion of the house, Charly thanked Mr. Baker for his hospitality and, when invited, stated she would like to come again simply to go to. And she intended it. She sensed the loneliness in him and decided he in all likelihood did not have many site visitors.Back on the street again, she suppressed the urge to invite, "How did I do?" Her mind turned into already reviewing the next farms and then there was the hassle of lunch. By the time they reached their next destination, it would be 12:30 and now was not a great time to disturb a farmer.Making her selection, she drove into Belleville and parked in the lot of her favored pizza parlor. It wasn't crowded but as it was simplest 11:30, so they didn't should anticipate a desk. She failed to ask McKinnon what his preferences had been and she did not virtually care. She usually ate a salad for lunch and she or he knew this was one eating place with a respectable salad bar.Once seated across from him, Charly commenced experiencing uncomfortable. He became so dammed uncommunicative and this was abruptly a social state of affairs. It had been tremendously smooth to push aside his presence till now. But there he sat, large as life, just across the small desk, studying the menu.Knowing precisely what she wanted, Charly did not want to look at the menu. So she looked at him rather and she saw him for the first time as a very appealing male. He could be mid-thirties and his capabilities were rugged, in preference to classically good-looking. His eyes were dark velvety-brown, included in the interim with the aid of the sweep of long and barely curled lashes. His hair became dark mahogany with reddish highlights, and it changed into just a little longer than the common cut.Too terrible the persona is the pits, she mused, after which nearly died while he glanced up sharply, and stared properly into her eyes. Almost as though he ought to study my mind, rattling it. She regarded away as the waitress approached, and quickly gave her order for the salad bar and espresso.Muttering, "Excuse me, please," she left the table and made her manner to the Ladies' room. How embarrassing to be stuck staring at him, like a schoolgirl! No doubt he is doing his great to unnerve me, however, he is not going to be triumphant. I want this process and I'm going to get it.The self-administered pep communication was regarded to help, and he or she made her way to the salad bar, in which she piled her plate with all her favorite matters. As she seated herself at their desk, she observed that McKinnon turned into ingesting a steak sandwich and idea, fits you, and once more looked down speedy as he once more glanced sharply at her.This is ridiculous! We're two grown human beings, having lunch together, and I'm acting like an idiot. Have I been given to interrupting the ice one way or the other, however how? He hates girls, he solves questions in monosyllables and he doesn't want me to have this activity. Oh, the hell with it. I may be impolite too.Ignoring him absolutely, she proceeded to devour her lunch, reviewing the subsequent two farms in her thoughts. Once mentally involved, it turned into smooth to hold on even though she had been alone. The subsequent two farms were dairy and pork, respectively, and she or he should see no cause why both have to pose any hassle. But no doubt there have been troubles, or he would not have selected them."You failed to inform us you have been getting married, Miss Benson." The declaration introduced her quickly out of her reverie, and she or he without delay observed his eyes once more fixed on her left hand."That's due to the fact I'm now not, Mr. McKinnon." And besides, it would not manifest to be any of your rattling commercial enterprises anyway. Again, he seemed sharply at her, and over again, she had the feeling he may want to read her thoughts."Sorry. My mistake." And he returned to his meal, as though he hadn't spoken. But she caught him looking at numerous extra instances on the diamond on her left hand.Glancing at her watch, she finished her espresso and was planning to depart, while McKinnon ordered a chunk of coconut cream pie, and he or she turned compelled to take a seat and wait whilst he ate it.Slowly, it regarded her.Paying for the meal on the way out, Charly asked for a receipt and filed it away. Once hired, she would be allowed costs for mileage and food, so why now not assume definitely and begin now? She observed there has been no comment from her shadow.The next farm changed into well-maintained, but it seemed that the majority of the money went into the barns, devices, and outbuildings. As she approached the house, Charly observed the beds of stunning roses, but the construction become antique and needed a little paint to freshen it up.The motive for McKinnon's desire changed into obvious as soon because the door become responded. The farmer's spouse was younger and pretty and in all likelihood never obsessed with every other younger girl going into the barn together with her husband. Well, no problem. After introducing herself and explaining her presence, Charly positioned her left hand as much as her hair to push it again, turning barely so the sun could capture her ring. At the same time, she commented on the roses with genuine interest, due to the fact she had been supporting them along with her Dad's bushes for years. As the dialogue moved from insurance examining to roses and rings, Charly sensed McKinnon shifting off out of listening to variety. Tough luck, McKinnon. Foiled once more. Mrs. Gordon became quite friendly now and apologized to Charly due to the fact her husband changed into in town, and will she do her inspecting without him? Charly assured her that would be no problem and were given on with it. McKinnon observed silently.Climbing around via barns became not anything new to Charly, but doing so dressed as she changed into, become a nuisance. She hated having to be aware of her apparel all the time and vowed this will be the last day she was dressed inappropriately. It might be less complicated to get at the wiring to check it greater cautiously if she becomes in blue jeans, as she could be at domestic. Oh nicely, the following day changed into any other day.Her notes and pics were taken, Charly back to the motive force's seat of the SUV, ignoring McKinnon as he again folded his length into the tight quarters. She replaced the Gordons' document and withdrew the subsequent one, glanced on the map, and commenced the engine. He buckled up his belt and proceeded to stare out via the windshield.Driving to the next farm, Charly had a while to surprise him. How could absolutely everyone stay silent for goodbye and be so gloomy? It just wasn't natural. Why all of the animosity towards her? Although she had a strong feeling it wasn't simply her. She'd be willing to guess he treated all women with the identical distant dislike.Being a very outgoing person herself, Charly turned into locating it increasingly hard to remain silent, however, knew herself nicely sufficient to understand that if she began a communique and he failed to respond, she might likely grow to be being very rude. And she couldn't come up with the money to be just now. So she held her tongue and drove on.

# CHAPTER TWO

A marvel awaited her on the ultimate farm of the day. When the door changed opened, an antique school buddy, with whom she had lost contact, greeted her enthusiastically. She ought to almost experience McKinnon snorting with derision as they swiftly chatted approximately the years they had misplaced. She intentionally extended the communique an extra little while.After promising to go back on her days off someday for a real go-to, Charly finished the inspection. She become aware that McKinnon had perched himself towards a bale of hay and was letting her get on with it with the aid of herself. Could that imply he turned into starting to trust her, or changed into just checking out her? She wasn't involved due to the fact she knew her inspections had been thorough and professional.Overall, the day had been simpler than she had anticipated. The actual work gave her no purpose for fear. Her only worry was that McKinnon might locate some cause to justify now not giving her the job. So ways, so true, and the next day changed into some other day.Charly walked back to wherein she had left McKinnon, only to discover that he had gone out of doors. Joining him by the car, she put her files collectively neatly and organized to depart. With the car over again out at the dual carriageway, she had time to examine her watch and experience thrilled that it turned into just after 5:00, despite her coffee smash inside the morning and her afternoon chats.Arriving lower back in the workplace at 5:30, Charly went into the now-empty construction with McKinnon to return the completed documents to the boardroom and select up to three greater for the following day. Still, he maintained his silence, speaking only whilst vital."We're staying at the Isle day after today, so we must end early." Handing her the files he had chosen, he turned to the door and waited along with his hand on the mild switch, till she left the room.Charly couldn't wait to get away from him. The `Isle' became Quinte's Isle, Prince Edward County, bordered via Lake Ontario and the Bay of Quinte. She had grown up on the Isle and knew many farmers who had been neighbors of her dad and mom while they have been farming, so it changed into pretty doable that she would know a number of the farms he had selected. Leaving the construction, she tossed a "See you the next day," over her shoulder, as she headed for her car.He didn't respond, just unlocked his Cadillac and was given in.With every other forty-five minutes pressure in advance of her, Charly took a minute to examine the file names. What success! Uncle Henry! Well, she knew for certain which farm she could go to first. And maybe she'd simply provide McKinnon something to consider whilst she was at it. Her mind changed into busy formulating plans for all of the manner homes, so the time surpassed quickly.The weather has been unseasonably hot for May and Charly knew the farmers have been looking ahead to a cold spell soon. Although she now lived near the town, she still stored an ear to the climate from addiction. The forecast is also referred to as rain and winds by way of mid-week from a hurricane front transferring up from the Eastern States. She had learned at a young age that the weather turned into one thing farmers had to take delivery of and work around.Studying the files that evening, she located them to be pretty unremarkable. Just farms. Perhaps McKinnon knew now that she could not be thrown. Or perhaps he knew something about them that she failed to. Asking her Dad for a fast rundown on the two other documents, she becomes assured that they were each pretty respectable and responsible." In truth, I assume Tom Harrison is a director for the agency, isn't he?" he asked Charly."I wager it's pretty viable. The day I changed into there, I became too busy trying to defend myself in opposition to McKinnon's attacks to take any observation of the others. Thanks, Dad. It would be much like him to throw in a director's document and hope I embarrassed myself."Now, Charly, he can not be all that bad. I don't know the man for my part, but I've never heard something against him. Are you positive you are not imagining matters?"Yeah, I suppose I'm simply paranoid because I need this task so badly." She dropped the situation and went to the telephone, her good humor restored as she thought of McKinnon's face the following day."Hi, Uncle Henry. Are you going to be domestic the next day? Yes? Will you do me a favor? I've were given to come over there with a filled shirt on enterprise and I want you to fake you don't know me until I provide you with a sign. Don't ask why. It's just a little funny story amongst friends. Okay?"After some muttering, her uncle finally agreed and they said their goodbyes. Charly turned into grinned as she prepared for bed. McKinnon never so much as batted a watch while he joined her the next morning in her automobile. She had donned Western boots, snug denim, and a semi-dressy western blouse and had tucked her hair up beneath her western hat. Outside of a short "Good morning," he became his common inscrutable self.It became just a quick force to her uncle's farm, and Charly ought to infrequently wait to get there. She jumped out of the SUV, picked up her clipboard, and headed over to wherein her uncle become running on a tractor engine. She swung her hips and made the maximum of her comfortable denim, understanding that McKinnon became following and watching. Her uncle straightened up as she approached, and she watched in amazement as he regarded beyond her, smiled, and stretched his hand out to McKinnon."T. G., how are you?" He asked, shaking arms with him. She appeared from one to the alternative, understanding all of sudden that her plan had one way or the other long past pretty wrong. As they talked to each different, ignoring her absolutely, she became irritated, then enraged. Turning her return on them, she yanked her hat from her head, forgetting about her hair. As it tumbled in glowing auburn waves to her waist, she stomped into the barn, leaving the others wherein they had been. She was unaware of the gleam in McKinnon's eye as he watched her development. Her uncle had he returned to the barn, so saw simplest the admiration on T. G.'s face, now not the purpose for it.Hurrying via the inspection, Charly wrote up her notes after which set the document aside. Working speedy, she braided her hair and fixed it up as it has been the day passed. The laugh hadn't even commenced and already it was over. Serves me proper for trying to get the higher of him. When she approached the guys once more, she discovered they had been deep in conversation, however, stopped speaking as quickly as they noticed her presence."Everything seems to be in order, Mr. McKinnon. I'd like to get directly to the subsequent one if you don't thoughts. Goodbye, Mr. Thomas."Throwing an arm around her shoulders, her uncle squeezed her and said, "You don't need to fake you do not know me, Charly. T. G. Already knew we were related. Good good fortune with your activity. I realize you'll make a great inspector."Feeling like a little female again, Charly muttered "Goodbye," again and headed for the automobile. McKinnon sauntered alongside behind, grinning widely.Back in the car, Charly attempted to get herself beneath manage. As soon as, he had the upper hand and she or he failed to like the feeling. To make matters worse, the next farm becomes Harrison's.Should she come right out and ask if he becomes a director? It might make her appearance even greater silly. Maybe she'd recognize him while she noticed him. Deciding to stay quiet, she drove off, hoping for the first-class.She did understand him as quickly as he appeared. He had been one of the ones who had spoken up in her defense on several instances throughout the interview. Relaxing immediately, Charly chatted away with him as they toured his buildings and tested the wiring. The farm turned into an amazing circumstance and glaringly paid for itself. But she checked the whole lot over, understanding there have been administrators watching her now.It became once more lunchtime once they were finished, and she determined to force over to Bloomfield, before preventing for lunch. It become a small village but had a splendid eating place, and the third farm changed into simply outside of the city. With her salad in front of her, Charly has become eaten up using her curiosity. T. G. McKinnon. Tom Gregory? Timothy George? Terry Glenn? None of them suit, and she or he just could not stand it any longer."What does the T. G. Stand for?" She looked across the desk at McKinnon and wondered if he might solution her, or maintain his normal stony silence."My mother stated it stood for `Thank God, because she had three daughters and my Dad would not give up till he had a son. My start certificate says Thomas Gordon, however, I have to observe it now and then to bear in mind because I've never been something but T. G. Satisfied?" He became almost smiling, as even though he knew she was sitting there trying to pin a name on him."Yes, thanks." Returning to her salad, she determined that T. G. Perfect him better. He certainly wasn't a Thomas, perhaps a Gordon; alternatively, perhaps now not. And he had said several sentences to her. Wow - a primary breakthrough! Her silent contemplation was interrupted when he requested, "And Charly? That's not precisely a female call."Short for Charlene, but I turned into carrying denim overalls and trailing Dad around the barn from the time I should stroll, so Charly I became. And still am." She regarded up at him as she spoke and found his eyes on her mouth. They have been now not indifferent or bloodless, however only for a second. He masked his expression quickly and remarked approximately how early they would be through these days, barring any unexpected circumstances.Again selecting up the tab, Charly vowed there might be none. She was beginning to sense as though she'd been inspecting farms for weeks in preference to days. And she additionally felt that McKinnon had misplaced most of his reservations approximately her.The day ended early and without incident. The temperature become nonetheless unseasonably high and the climate turned beginning to be oppressive. She became satisfied to get home and take an extended hot bath, before reading the documents for the following day. Tomorrow - the day that might decide her whole destiny. On one hand, she became quite positive she had the activity, however, on the other, she nonetheless doubted that McKinnon sincerely desired her in the workforce. Maybe today he has been friendlier so that she could loosen up and allow her to guard down tomorrow.However, Wednesday morning found Charly dressed in a faded blue jumpsuit, her hair smartly braided and fixed to the back of her head. Her boots were wiped clean and polished and she or he looked and felt like a professional. The farms they have been searching at nowadays have been on the other facet of Belleville for a long way, so it might be an extended day.McKinnon appeared to be in good humor while she picked him up from the office. He become smiling as he stated desirable morning, and after a quick look at her outfit, stated, "Much more suitable attire, Miss Benson."I'm satisfied you approve because this could be my fashionable uniform anymore." "Oh, you've got been employed, have you?"Blushing, she glanced sideways, and become amazed to peer a touch of humor in his smile. Maybe he wasn't such a crammed blouse despite everything. Sighing inaudibly, she pulled out into the visitors and decided to revel in herself.Easier stated than finished, she mused, as one after some other, the farmers proceeded to whinge to her approximately the coverage they carried, the prices they had to pay, the claims that were settled unfairly, of their opinion, till her head was swimming. She knew that she have to continue to be dependable to the company at all expenses, but she didn't want to alienate any customers.Surprisingly, McKinnon came to her rescue in numerous events. He became informed and reasonable, and they seemed to appreciate his opinion. Maybe they just assume I do not know whatever due to the fact I'm a lady. Pushing the terrible thought apart, she executed her inspections, conscious that the climate was turning even sultrier.During lunch, extreme hurricane caution became issued for the area northeast of Belleville. Charly determined to rush through the following inspection, understanding that McKinnon changed into in all likelihood irritating to get domestic. There was sure to be a backlash of rain and wind on the Isle. With the radio on, they listened to the updates as they drove to their next vacation spot. The farm became located on a returned avenue pretty a long way from Belleville and wound through heavy bush. The timber was still, the sky a dull metal grey.On attaining the farm, Charly failed to waste any time. She asked her questions, ran thru her inspection, and made her notes. She didn't skip any areas that wanted to be checked on, and because the milking gadget turned into an older one, she went over to have a higher observe the wiring at the milking machine motor housing. McKinnon had observed her around and turned into status over using the window. She leaned ahead to test the wires, her again to him, and all at once felt a jolt of sexual tension run through her. It became powerful, like a charge of electricity, and her body answered of its own accord.Straightening slowly, she turned and looked at McKinnon. He became staring out the window, however, the telltale flush alongside his cheekbones instructed her all she had to know. So. The guy wasn't as inhuman as he appeared. In reality, if that idea originated in his thoughts, and she or he knew it had, he becomes very human and prone to the sight of a girl's derriere in tight pants. Well, nicely, nicely!The farmer became worried approximately the climate as properly. He changed into letting the farm animals out of the backyard into an area away from the buildings and commencing home windows and doorways to the barns. Charly knew that for the reason that intense tornadoes in Woodstock and Barrie, farmers everywhere in the province took warnings of intense climate very seriously now. She failed to like the feel of the climate. It turned into too quiet, too nonetheless. Nothing stirred, but the sky had an eerie hue to it and a charisma that she could best describe as alive, although the clouds did not seem like moving.Joining McKinnon at the car, she requested, "Can we beat it home?"I desire so." Just three phrases, but she knew he doubted it. "Would you like me to drive?" "No thank you, if it's ok with you. When I'm frightened, I prefer to have something to do.And I do not thoughts telling you I'm anxious." As she completed talking, the radio crackled and the announcer counseled them that the warnings were up to date to tornado signals for Central and Eastern Ontario, to be in effect till at least 9:00 p.m.Ten miles down the road, Charly all at once commenced shivering. It wasn't cold inside the automobile, and she or he knew it had nothing to do with the temperature. She had had those warnings before. Stopping the auto, she turned to McKinnon and said, "Please don't ask any questions, and please do not interrupt me for a couple of minutes. There's something I have to take care of. Just bear with me." Closing her eyes, she took a couple of deep breaths and forced herself to loosen up totally. Years of meditation practice enabled her to close out all exterior influences and clean her mind. Envisioning the vehicle, T. G. And herself, she imagined a huge golden, impenetrable bubble around the car. She held the idea in her thoughts, and as a notable experience of peace got here over her, she opened her eyes.McKinnon turned into staring transfixed at her. Come to think of it, he had a reason. To abruptly forestall riding, ask him to be quiet after which sit returned together with her eyes shut, must make him assume she changed into dropping her sanity."Can I ask what that changed into all about?" He changed into still staring at her, a frown wrinkling his brow.Before she may want to form an answer, she saw his expression alternate and heard him swear. The SUV become packed with an unearthly roaring, and as they watched, timber slammed down into the road in the front of them. The vehicle rocked under the pressure of the wind and rain because it drove in opposition to them. Turning to the appearance at the back, she could not see an element. The windows have been streaming with water and the roar of the wind changed into deafening.Looking over at McKinnon, she noticed the white line around his mouth and his clenched fist because it rested at the dash. Feeling sudden compassion for him, she positioned her hand on his thigh for a moment. "It's okay, McKinnon. We won't be harmed."How can you understand that? Why aren't you terrified? Why did you stop the automobile when you did? We nearly got wiped out." His phrases came out jerky and grim at the identical time."I can't explain it right now. Maybe later. Just trust me that we're going to be secure. The hurricane might not touch us." She quickly withdrew her hand from his thigh.As although to give credence to her phrases, the rain started to slacken, and the wind got here in bursts. With visibility now returned, they appeared out and couldn't agree with the devastation around them. Large timber and small have been uprooted and have been flung every which manner, a few in the front of the automobile, some at the back of it, but none touching it. They may want to see a swath cut through the bush and it regarded to the component, and go round the car, then preserve on.McKinnon stared at her for long moments. He appeared outdoor again on the destruction and then seemed lower back at her. "I do not know what you probably did simply now, however, I have a sense I owe you my life. How did you have to forestall the automobile? I failed to listen to an element."Please don't ask me right now, McKinnon. I do not have time. I should permit my mom to understand I'm okay. No interruptions, please."You can not try this. We do not have a cellphone sign right here."Please, no questions." Once extra, she did her deep respiration, cleared her thoughts, and focused on sending her mother the understanding that she changed into security. Letting the idea go, she waited a few seconds until she felt the message had been received, then opened her eyes, best to peer him staring at her once more."Are you a witch?"No, McKinnon. I'm now not a witch. And I simply will try and explain later. But right now, I assume we should try to parent out what to do subsequent. Unless I'm mistaken, we are going to be here for some time, like perhaps all night." Opening the auto door, he stepped out and looked around. The rain had stopped as fast as it had come, and just a few gusts of wind swirled around him.

Charly got out and seemed round too. It becomes incredible. The street changed blocked in each guideline, with many fallen timber, and he or she knew they would not be able to clear it.

# CHAPTER THREE

"I'm afraid your estimation of the state of affairs is proper, Miss Benson. We'll be here for the night." He failed to appear inside the least glad at the chance.Knowing it might be an extended night within the confines of her small SUV, Charly cautioned they stay outside for a while and stretch their legs whilst they may. The hurricane had abated totally, although there has been nevertheless a low cloud cowl shifting rapidly overhead."Let's climb over the bushes and have to examine the road from the other aspect. Are you game?"She challenged him with the question, understanding it was a bit unfair due to the fact he was again wearing get-dressed pants, blouse, tie, blazer, and loafers."Oh sure, I'm recreation, Miss Benson. Let's cross."Progress turned gradual as they tried to make their way over and beneath and around trunks and branches of timber. Some nevertheless had roots attached with earth clinging to them, torn from the ground like matchsticks. Finally crawling via to some distance facet of the blockage, they stood looking up the street to every other mess of bushes in the distance, additionally blocking off the road."One night right here may be a barely positive estimate, Miss Benson." McKinnon had his fingers in his pockets and, as she becomes just in the back of him, she had a great hazard to respect his firm hips, the fabric of his trousers stretched tightly throughout them.Moving up beside him, she advised with a bit of luck, "Maybe the other aspect isn't always so badly blocked. Want to come back and notice?"Why no longer? There simply isn't much else to do. Besides, we are already quite wet from climbing around this mess. Or hadn't you noticed?"She hadn't, no longer until he mentioned it. And abruptly Charly began to surprise at the wisdom of her movements. The temperature had dropped substantially with the advent of the twister and it might be a long night. Making their way returned to the auto changed into a piece less difficult and as soon as there, she modified her thoughts approximately exploring similarly. In reality, the automobile turned into beginning to look like a higher area to be, with every passing minute.Once internal, she commenced the engine and grew to become the heater on complete strength. Then she fiddled with the radio until she located the Belleville station. As information about the devastation reached them, they listened in silence, thinking and demanding approximately their family and buddies. The reviews made no point out of the Isle. Most of the damage was to the northeast cease of the town and outlying areas. There were no fatalities reported as but and, on the whole, it seemed less extreme than the Barrie tornado."Well, I wager I can count on my property being safe. What approximately your family?" "Southwest cease of the metropolis. I imagine they're secure if they have been at domestic."Well, Miss Benson, in which would you want to dine this evening? I changed into going to take you out to dinner to have fun with your new function as our Farm Inspector, but it looks like a way to just wait. By the way, you are appropriate at your process and you'll be an asset to the company. My apologies for the difficult time I gave you the alternative day, but there had been extenuating instances."Apologies popular and I thank you. Getting this role manner an extremely good deal to me, Mr. McKinnon, and I won't assist you or the company down. As to dinner, all is not lost."Climbing out of the SUV, she went to the again and removed her `care' bundle, as she referred to it. Her Dad had provided it to her when she had bought the automobile and she had carried it around ever because. There becomes a vehicle rug, a sound asleep bag, and a box. She tossed the rag and slumbering bag into the second seat and carried the field again to the driving force's seat with her."This is one advantage of being an only toddler and female. Fathers generally tend to fear extra and be extra shielding."Shutting off the car engine, she took out four cans of liquids - grape, V-8, apple, and orange. Next was a massive bottle of dried fruit and nuts, and lastly, another large bottle jammed with granola bars, nevertheless in their wrappers."Dinner is served, Mr. McKinnon. If there may be any risk that we are going to be here a lot of past breakfast, we will preserve this stuff, but at the least, we might not pass hungry. Sorry I can not provide a hot meal."Believe me, Miss Benson, this seems like a royal banquet. I'm now not very good at going to bed hungry. By the way, are you able to drop Mr. McKinnon and speak to me T. G.? Formality appears a chunk ludicrous below the occasions, don't you observe?"Glancing at him, she changed into amazed to look at an actual smile lighting his face. The trade-in he was quite first-rate, as even though the hurricane had released him from a few emotional jails."As you desire, T. G., although I've been deliberating you as McKinnon for three days now, so I can also slip once in a while."Just

McKinnon? No Mr.? How unprofessional, Miss Benson!"Not most effective smiling, but nearly truly flirting. She thought he was coming into existence with a vengeance." Which sort of juice might you like, T. G.?" she asked, and smiled when he chose the grape."Maybe I can believe it's a completely young wine. And you?"Oh, I'm in reality a V-8 person. If I had made up this field, it would have been all V-eight. Although I assume one should get tired of that, given a protracted enough duration of isolation. And that reminds me; I ought to have a word with pricey antique Dad. By placing this stuff in my vehicle, he set up the expectation of my becoming stranded and perhaps even caused it. He ought to realize higher at his age. Oh nicely, I guess I can forgive him this time." "I won't pretend to apprehend what you just said, Charly, however, I thank your dad from the lowest of my heart. I'm starving."Why don't you do away with your tie, unbutton multiple buttons on that shirt, and act like you are home by way of your fire, relaxing?" Shaking a handful of fruit and nuts out for herself, she provided him the jar, adding, "You do have a hearth at domestic, do not you?" I do, yes. But how did you know that?"Because you appear like a hearth person." Popping cashew in her mouth, she watched as he pulled off the tie and stuffed it into his blazer pocket. He unbuttoned three buttons on his shirt, giving her a glimpse of a hair-darkened chest and a gold chain gleaming at his neck. Finding their courting changing a touch too hastily for her liking, Charly started to invite him questions about the employer she now labored for. He responded freely enough, till she came to one which threw him."Why did your remaining inspector depart, T. G.?"

She felt him stiffen beside her before the query become finished and knew come what may she had entered the forbidden territory. He became silent for so long she turned into positive he wasn't going to reply, then commenced to speak."He changed into fired. You see, Miss Benson, he turned into spending time examining my expensive spouse while he becomes purported to be out examining farms. When he left, she went with him. End of tale."Oh, McKinnon, I'm sorry. I wouldn't have dreamed of asking if I'd recognized." Charly wished with all her coronary heart that she'd accomplished some research into the administrators earlier than now. She felt as though she have been a Peeping Tom, searching into his existence in a manner that became none of her business."Don't be sorry, Charly. I'm simplest telling you this because you're going to pay attention to it from a person else, and I'd like you to recognize the fact. The marriage becomes a mistake from the beginning. We had been both too younger and didn't have any idea what we were getting into. I desired children, and she desired the birthday celebration. He wasn't the first guy she'd had an affair with, but it was the first time she was so blatantly indiscreet."He chewed on a chunk of dried apple, then endured, "Anyway, we've been divorced for a year now, and except for the anger that stays at her betrayal, I'm an awful lot happier living alone."Tearing the wrapper from a granola bar, he bit a chunk off, then asked, "What approximately that diamond on your left hand? I've bared my soul. Now it is your turn. Besides, I have a concept about it and I'd want to understand if I'm proper."Charly shifted slightly to try to get cushier. Damn small motors anyway!"First I want to invite you something, McKinnon. You picked the first three files due to the fact they were that maximum probably to purpose my issues, didn't you?" Her query turned into greater curious than accusatory.He grinned as he responded to her. "Guilty. I figured if you may cope with Baker and a couple of young wives, you would make it. I changed into right." "Then you need to recognize the hoop is for the benefit of the young better halves. It belonged to my Grandmother. I didn't come into this process with my eyes closed, and I knew adverse wives can be a trouble. The ring might not pacify all of them, but it's going to help a little."What approximately lecherous guys? Have you thought of that? "Oh, sure. And organized for it too. There changed into a very good Judo faculty in Hamilton and I was given my black belt. I'm no longer worried."Although it was too darkish to peer now, Charly felt his opinion of her upward push numerous notches. Finishing her granola bar and V-8, she tidied away the food. Reaching across in the front of McKinnon, she took the flashlight from the glove compartment."Okay, T. G., who's first for the toilet? It's pretty massive, genuinely, however, would not have a shower."Giggling, she corrected her announcement quickly. "Well, it did have, however, we have missed it."Judo or not, I'll move first, in case you do not mind. God is aware of what the storm stirred up within the bush. He climbed out of the car and she found out it turned a lot chillier now.While he was long gone, Charly tipped the seats again as some distance as they might pass, thankful for the recliners. She placed the rug on his and pulled the napping bag as much as hers. After all, he had a blazer. She just had her long-sleeved jumpsuit.When he again, she took the flashlight from him and requested, "Any beasties obtainable?" "None that I could see, however, do be long.

This is rabies us of a." Thanks, McKinnon. You realize a way to put a person's thoughts at rest. See you."The jumpsuit she had found so snug and expert now have become an intensive nuisance as she attempted to keep it out of the most timber. And the air changed into bloodless! She returned to the car in report time, to discover McKinnon stretched out on his reclining seat, his blazer off and folded for a pillow. He had additionally removed his footwear and had unfolded the blanket over his legs. His blouse sleeves had been rolled lower back to his elbows, and despite the cramped quarters, he appeared quite cushy."This resort isn't always bad, Miss Benson. I might even deliver it three stars in my assessment."It is not morning yet, McKinnon, so don't be too hasty. The beds do not depart lots of room for tossing and turning. In reality, I think it'd be secure to mention turning might be out of the question."Removing her shoes, Charly settled herself into her sound asleep bag, looking to get cushty below the steerage wheel."You have more room than I ever have, T. G., however, you furthermore might have an extra body to set up, so I wager we're even."It turned darkish now, and Charly could see nothing. She changed into quite snug in her sleeping bag, and having business enterprise whilst she turned into stranded became an additional bonus. He genuinely changed into a pretty human."It's too early to sleep but, Charly, how about telling me what you have been doing at some stage in the typhoon? I've been very patient up until now." "Agreed. You were patient and I knew you have been going to invite me, but I still do not know how tons or how little I'm going to inform you. It just isn't always something I'm snug talking about to maximum human beings."Why don't you simply start at the beginning and spot what happens? Believe me, I'll be an attentive target market, as well as a captive one."Okay, McKinnon. But please take into account, that this isn't smooth for me. How plenty do you realize about metaphysics?"You imply séances, witchcraft, black magic, and stuff like that?"No, I don't. I imply dream evaluation, reincarnation, non-secular realm as an actual a part of the physical realm, telepathy, and so forth."I study a chunk approximately years ago, however, I discarded maximum of it as someone's fantasy. Except for reincarnation, this is. I need extra information, however, it makes feel to me."Well, after I became approximately five, my mother and father joined a metaphysical have a look at the institution. They introduced domestic a series of training cassette tapes on meditation, dream analyses, holistic recovery, and so on., and played them again and again. I guess I absorbed an extremely good deal of it because I started having precognitive desires when I turned about seven. They had been about fires, aircraft crashes, vehicle injuries, and stuff like that. The dreams usually happened about a week before the incident. When I might listen approximately it, I would turn out to be very dissatisfied, I bet questioning that I should be able to prevent them from taking place. But I in no way knew wherein they had been taking vicinity, just that they were going to happen."My parents commenced taking me to the conferences so that I could higher understand what turned into occurring. Soon the precognitive desires stopped, however now not the alternative dreams. I learned how to investigate the symbols in my dreams so that I may want to recognize my behavior and exchange what wished changing. I also become capable of getting solutions to questions or troubles through dream evaluation. It's simply too sizable a topic for me to get into proper now, but you spend one-third of your existence dozing and an extraordinary deal of that point dreaming. There is so much know-how and know-how to be received from goals, you could not begin to guess at the extent of the advantages."I think the single maximum essential factor that I discovered from the observed institution become the truth that thoughts on the bodily aircraft are deeds, or matters, at the spiritual one. I realize it sounds notable and a completely difficult concept to grasp without the heritage take a look at, however, it is the basis for what I become doing this afternoon."First of all, I stopped the car due to the fact I unexpectedly got a chilly sit back. To me, that intended that we had been in intense threat. Now comes the element you will have a problem with. I honestly positioned myself into a meditative nation, something else I found out at a completely young age, and predicted a huge, golden ball of light strength around the car, you and I. I held the thought for a minute or so. It's a bit like generating a superb force area, but there's no way I can show that it works. My parents and I had been doing this for years, in the course of blizzards, whilst one person became taking place a journey, and we've never been in injuries. Makes us feel good besides. Today changed into the first real demonstration of a fantastic reaction."Pausing, she glanced at him then asked, "Have I very well burdened you?"Not entirely, however, you've got sincerely given me an excellent deal to consider. I may get my books out and feature some others to have a look at them. It feels like an exciting way to spend a rainy day."That's the humorous component approximately it,

McKinnon. If your mind accepts the theories, it will become a manner of life and you find each factor of your lifestyle modifications. It turns into not being possible to lie, cheat, or harm all of us in any manner, via concept, word, or deed. I changed into so younger once I became brought to it all, I simply assumed that everyone knew and practiced this stuff. But after I attempted to talk to the opposite youngsters at school, they laughed at me. Up till today, I have not discussed it with anybody but my mother and father. Thanks for listening. It turned into true to talk approximately it."So one may say you're a very good witch?"You're without a doubt determined to make me out to be a witch, are not you, McKinnon? Okay, right here's a few witchcraft for you. Think of something you want, however, don't tell me what it's far. As quickly as you get domestic tomorrow, write it out on a piece of paper and seal the paper in an envelope with the date on it. Then write on any other piece of paper the following words: My conscious thoughts accept the truth that I chose and deserve the following: then you upload whatever it's that you need. And it can be something from changing an awful dependency to obtaining a gold watch. When you write it out make certain to put in writing `I have, not `I want, as though it had been already a fact."Now, for the next thirty-three days, you write the same factor out just earlier than going to sleep. Then watch for the outcomes. One element it's miles particularly top for is education yourself to take into account your dreams."Here's every other exercise for you. Sit back, close your eyes, and follow my commands. You are approximate to be introduced to the maximum powerful force in the world. It's called the Universal Law of Attraction and it applies to anybody, all of the time."Imagine that there is an effective magnet inside your core of you. Whether it consists of a positive or a bad price relies upon you – your mind - but on the whole your emotions. Then believe that the Universe is a large shopping center. You could have whatever you need – correct health, cash, healthy relationships, a new automobile, or new furniture. You are best restricted through your feelings of self-esteem, your imagination, and your capability to accept as true."Suppose you'd like to have twenty-five thousand bucks. Visualize a huge bubble. Inside of the bubble, see yourself maintaining a cheque for five thousand bucks. See the huge smile on your face, feel the glad feeling in your intestine."You have simply created an occasion so that it will take area, depending on how badly you want it, and provided you maintain your inner magnet positively charged. Once an afternoon, take a few minutes to visualize the bubble once more and feel the pleasure preserving that cheque will convey to you. See a shimmering inexperienced light like the Northern Lights, surrounding the bubble, turning more potent and larger on every occasion you exercise the technique. Then thank the Universe for giving it to you, as though you have already got it, and allow it to go. It isn't your responsibility to determine how this could come approximately – that's the activity of the Universe. It is handiest up to you to sense worthy and to agree with. You can open your eyes now."One of the quickest and first-rate methods to generate and hold a superb rate for your internal magnet is to provide gratitude and thank you, as soon as an afternoon, for at the least seven things for which you are thankful. What you recognition on is what you carry to yourself, be it poverty or wealth, infection or precise fitness, disappointment or happiness. The Law of Attraction is continually working so we should be aware of what we're bringing to ourselves."When it involves health, something is fixable, the use of simplest your mind. I understand that sounds incredible, however, there are many documented cases in which human beings have cured themselves of 'incurable' diseases, without medical intervention. When you realize that your complete body is composed of completely new cells approximately every seven years, it stands to purpose that you may replace diseased cells with healthful ones, absolutely using focusing on fitness in place of contamination. As the diseased cells are changed with healthful ones, your fashionable condition gradually improves, till you are well. The trick is to focus on health, give no thought or power to the infection, and give thank you each day for the recovery."Anyway, I think that's greater than sufficient for one lesson. We had higher get a little sleep in case we've got a ten-mile walk within the morning."I think you're proper, however, it isn't always going to be easy after everything you've advised me. My mind is busy looking to procedure all of it."Settling herself greater with ease, Charly yawned, stretched, and muttered, "Shut up, McKinnon." The day has been long and exhausting, however now she was heat, comfortable and satisfied, and equipped to fall asleep."Goodnight to you too, Charly." He additionally shifted to try and settle extra without problems. Silence settled over them.Charly becomes simply started to go to sleep whilst she started to experience her body come alive with sexual emotions and sensations. She had been considering the those who were now homeless from the twister and about the cleanup that might take days and weeks. So she knew that the mind had been coming from McKinnon. She attempted to shut her thoughts off, however, it became vain. As her desire grew, she may wanted to nearly consider him making like to her, and the warmth that started to flash through her body threatened to make her do something she would regret in the morning. Knowing she had to forestall him at once, she became her head in his route, and spoke softly."McKinnon, are you wide awake?"Hmm. You want something?" She could inform from his response that he was on the verge of sleep.Clearing her throat, she pulled her mind together. "There are multiple different things I need to have advised you, McKinnon. As I simply informed you, all of us have power fields and magnetic electricity. There are approximately thirty-six extraordinary frequencies of energy. When human beings are nicely mated, their power fields balance and decorate every different. I have a motive to accept as true with we are on complimentary wavelengths, McKinnon. I also ought to have advised you that psychic power and sexual power are so similar that the difference between them is almost non-existent."Sighing, she asked, "Would you please close your mind down, or think about something else? For a few purposes, I'm choosing up photographs from you - no specifics, simply fashionable emotions. It's no longer exactly conducive to sleep. And I apologize for intruding, but on occasion, this stuff shows up and I haven't any manipulate over them."You are a witch. But the truth that I become considering making love to you is mostly your fault. You walked round in front of me sporting tight denim, and also you let your glorious hair tumble down your lower back while you knew I become watching. I'm sorry for keeping you wakeful, however, believe me, I became having a very good time."Oh, I trust you, McKinnon. I changed into there as properly. Remember? Anyway, fall asleep. We'll maybe talk this further once more."Once extra, quiet settled over the automobile. Charly closed her eyes and settled down greater snugly into her dozing bag. Then she simply had to say one greater component."You're an ok guy, McKinnon." "So are you, Charly. So are you."

# CHAPTER FOUR

Waking to a brilliant and sunny morning, Charly at once appeared over at McKinnon, to locate that he turned into looking her with a half-smile on his face."Hi, Witch," he stated softly."Hi, yourself," she responded, grinning, aware that she felt no embarrassment over closing night time's thoughts reading. Her hair had come loose inside the night, and she should feel his eyes wandering over it because it lay in a tangled mass around her shoulders."Would you mind if we convey the Caddy next time?"Not at all, however, can we provide you with a much less unfavorable excuse for being stranded?" Leering at her, McKinnon drawled, "I could usually run out of fuel."To get right down to commercial enterprise, how lengthy earlier than we get dug out of here, do you think?"Well, I suggest we take a hike back off the road after breakfast and notice how sizeable the damage is there. We already understand it's very horrific beforehand folks."McKinnon had thrown off the rug, straightened the seat up, and changed into changing his shoes. "Guess you don't have any shaving tools with you, huh?"Just one extra motive why you ought to have employed a person." She smiled at him, taking part in the possibility to tease him."No thanks. I'm turning used to our little female Inspector."The blockage on the street at the back of the auto was almost as horrific as the only one in the front.

After a few dialogues, they determined they could as well wait it out. As though it turned into a sign that they had made the proper decision, a helicopter flew over, rotated returned, and dipped at them, to allow them to know that they had been visible. When they had struggled lower back through the fallen bushes to the auto, Charly opened her briefcase and eliminated more than one sheet of clean paper."Know how to play battleships, McKinnon? "Sure. But it is been approximately twenty years since I remaining did it." "No hassle. Make your grid with ten squares, numbered from one to ten across the pinnacle and A to J down the aspect. I assume it is a five-square destroyer, a four-square submarine, and more than one little three-rectangular something-or-others."Okay. First, one to sink all of the different's boats wins, proper?" "Right."They settled down to play, concentrating on the game and the struggle of wits. But Charly had forgotten how tons in music with each other they have been and realized nearly right away that McKinnon becomes studying her thoughts to select off her boats, simply as she becomes studying his. The first recreation ended nearly as quickly because it had begun."So McKinnon, you now not handiest send messages telepathically, you receive them as well. I informed you we were well matched. Now we can create new strategies." Charly figured she nonetheless had a bonus over McKinnon due to the fact she had regularly attempted to apply her mental powers in games earlier than with greater than a little achievement. But this time, she couldn't trust it when he sank all of her boats in file time. She had the handiest one hit on his boats and one small one sunk."How did you do that?" Pure logic. I knew you would be concentrating on blank squares, so I overlooked what I became choosing up from you. Then I sincerely focused on my boats, hoping you would expect that I turned into thinking of clean squares as properly."Very smart, McKinnon, very smart. Want to strive for one greater?" But the subsequent game never occurred, for just then they heard, in reality, the sound of a heavy engine. Charly watched as McKinnon helped the road group clean the trees with chain saws and axes. She might have provided help as nicely, but knew they might refuse.When one of the people commented on the truth that they had been very lucky, Charly threw a warning glance at McKinnon, and he just agreed that they'd indeed been lucky.The drive again to Picton appeared to bypass in no time. There turned into this sort of feeling of kinship with McKinnon now that Charly determined it very difficult to consider he turned into her superior, although the supervisor became her immediate boss. They had installed a close rapport final night, and it become not possible to go again to their former sterile relationship.It appeared that McKinnon felt the identical manner. "I need you to vow me something, Charly. I won't be going out examining with you anymore, so if you have troubles with all of us, I want you to allow me to know immediately. We've informed the workplace group of workers not to take any verbal abuse from all and sundry - clients or brokers. So now I'm telling you the equal component. If everyone offers you a difficult time approximately their coverage, you refer them to the supervisor or one of us. Just don't allow them to be rude to you. You'll be a little extra uncovered to that kind of factor than the women within the office, so you'll have a greater problem dealing with it. They can constantly hang up the phone.

Promise?"Promise, McKinnon. And thank you. I may not deny that there can be issues of that nature. I saw it the day before today. But if I go out without the expectancy of strolling into it, it may not occur." "More witchcraft?" No, simply high-quality thinking, every other issue that works very powerfully, if humans however knew it. As I advised you earlier, thoughts are things so that you do deliver to yourself something you focus upon."Looking over at her with a half-grin, McKinnon stated, "Will you have got dinner with me in the close future, Charly? Call it a belated celebration of your hiring, however truly I want to speak to you greater about these things."Perhaps. I expect we'll be too busy for a while, although. There's going to be several cleansing as much as coping with. And I imagine your Claims Adjustor could be run off his ft for the following while."Her phrases proved to be especially true. Everyone in the workplace changed into pressed into the carrier as facts became amassed, assembled, and claims have been sorted out and handled. Most of the hurricane victims had discovered haven by the time Charly and McKinnon had lower back to civilization.Friday afternoon she become just leaving the office whilst she noticed McKinnon on foot towards her. Pausing on the steps, she waited for him to attain her."How are you holding up, Charly? "Fine, McKinnon. I heard you had been busy working with the cleanup crews. How are they progressing?" Quite nicely. Hydro and phones have been restored, a maximum of the streets are open now, and people are starting to consider rebuilding. But there may be nonetheless masses to do. I'd like to take you out for that dinner tonight, in case you are unfastened."I may be, I bet. I'll need an hour to head home and get modified. What did you have in mind?"Something comfortable and quiet in Belleville. I've already got reservations for eight."Grinning at her, he endured, "You see I'm psychic too. I knew you'd say sure. I'll choose you up at 7:30."Don't get too sure of yourself, McKinnon. I may flip you into a frog."The faster the better, little witch. Then you may be obliged to kiss me to do away with the spell. See you later." And he ran down the steps to his vehicle, before she should think of a suitable retort.Charly dressed cautiously for her dinner date. She needed to admit that she changed into enthusiastic about the chance of eating with him. She enjoyed their conversations and the feeling of information that turned into growing between them.When McKinnon arrived, he got here in and visited along with her dad and mom for a couple of minutes. Charly fashionable the easy way he had with them and the truth that he seemed in no hurry to run off along with her.Driving to Belleville, he commented on how snug her dad and mom' domestic seemed to be. She questioned if he was unconsciously evaluating it on his very own, before his divorce. If what he had said approximately his spouse became true, she was certain his home must have been something but enjoyable.When the wine he ordered had been added to the desk, he toasted `our new little Inspector' and someway Charly did not thoughts being called little. It had often annoyed her within the beyond, especially at some stage in her college years.Once again, the restaurant lived as much as expected, and they talked little as they dined on escargot, filet mignon, baked potato, and asparagus pointers. As they relaxed over Spanish coffee, though, they fell into the easy verbal exchange, like old pals meeting after a lengthy separation."So, Little Farm Inspector, have you run into any troubles but?" Hardly,

McKinnon. I've been supporting inside the workplace in view that we were given domestic the other day. But I do have a problem. Can you tell me of any homes to hire, ideally out within the U. S. A.? I want to get out by myself now that I'm gainfully hired."You are a witch, Charly. And there's nothing you could say now so that it will persuade me in any other case." He become observing her again, with an expression of amused bafflement."What made you assert that? I just asked in case you knew of a house I should lease." She frowned at him, confused."Remember what you advised me about writing out something I wanted every night time for thirty-three nights?" Charly had forgotten, however, she smiled and asked, "What's that got to do with anything?"Open this and study it." Taking a small envelope from his internal breast pocket, he handed it to her. Wednesday's date was written at the outdoor of it and the envelope was sealed."Are you positive you need me to open this?"Indeed, I do. In reality, I wish you would hurry up."Shrugging her shoulders, Charly tore the end from the envelope. She pulled out a slip of paper and unfolded it. The phrases jumped from the web page.`I have an accountable, dependable tenant for the dwelling on my second farm.', the confirmation stated, written in a bold hand. She read it, then study it again."Now, do you see what I mean? Pure witchcraft. The residence becomes manifestly intended for you." He looked at her with an accusatory grin. "I idea you stated this would take thirty-three days."Usually, however now not constantly. It depends on the occasions, your potential to trust, and the needs of any other people involved in your request." She stopped speaking all at once after which asked, "Are you pronouncing which you have accommodation for me?"Available at once, affordable lease, most important appliances included, and all utilities paid. The former owners spent most of their capital fixing up the residence. It's a thirty-year-old bungalow, and they renovated it completely. Then they'd multiple negative years with their coins plants and finally had to consider affirming bankruptcy. I passed off to pay attention that they were in trouble, so offered to buy them out for an honest market price. The conventional, and there I turned into a beautiful second domestic sitting empty. I changed into almost geared up to pay a person to appear after it for me. When are you able to flow in?" "How about Sunday afternoon? I don't have a whole lot except my clothes and some necessary gadgets like a bed, kitchen desk and chairs, and my pc and desk left over from my apartment days in Guelph. I suppose my mother has a few pieces of furniture she's been saving inside the basement for some years in case I ever did circulate out."Would you like me to help with the circulation? I have a truck we will use."That's one offer I may not even hesitate over. Of course, you may assist. I'm sure my Dad can be very appreciative. Now, inform me all about the residence. How many bedrooms, is there a den, laundry, what color are the carpets? I cannot wait to peer it." It was simply beginning to sink in that she might quickly have her own domestic and she or he turned into getting extra excited via the instant."That's no hassle. I'll take you over for a grand tour right now if you want." "Oh, consider me, I like!" She changed into impatient to be off.The house became all he had stated and more. It changed into very apparent to her that the former proprietors had spent an extraordinary deal of cash, due to the fact the wiring changed into newly up to date, and the oil furnace had been eliminated and changed with a heat pump and electric powered furnace. All of the rooms had been recently adorned in a colonial subject with warm autumn colors predominating. She hurried from one room to the next, examining the whole lot, and by the time she reached the den in the basement and discovered the hearth, she felt like she had simply come home. The room changed into painted with a touch of rose, and a cream rug on the ground. Off to one facet turned into a small powder room and laundry. The washer and dryer seemed new. The principal ground had three bedrooms, a rest room, a large USA kitchen, and a dwelling room. She already knew which bedroom might be her office and which one she might sleep in. McKinnon observed her around, taking pride in her satisfaction. He stood now, palms in pockets, looking at her as she flitted from room to room. "Would you don't forget to promote this house, McKinnon? You could sever a lot for me because I wouldn't need the land." "Why don't you just stay in it for a while and reflect on consideration on it, Charly? We can usually install a lease-to-purchase agreement, problem to severance if that is what you'd like. Would you try this? I bet once I reflect on consideration it, I'm now not in any function to buy till I pay returned a couple of loans. But that won't take long, after which I'll be asking you again." She nonetheless had trouble believing her precise fortune. McKinnon had perched himself on the edge of the bow window and his legs were extended in the front of him, crossed at the ankles. His arms had been once more in his trouser pockets, and his fit jacket changed into the open. Coming over to face beside him, she had her hands in her wallet as nicely. Pockets that she had hidden in the seams of her long dress. It becomes mild emerald green velvet with leg-of-mutton sleeves, excessive lace-trimmed collar, and tight-becoming waist. The lengthy skirt become A-line and the dress was certainly one of her favorites. She'd had many compliments on it but few human beings were conscious that she had made it herself. She had selected to wear her hair unfastened, pulled up on the sides, and secured with rhinestone combs. It fell in waves to her waist in the back. She knew that getting dressed gave her an old-fashioned air. How can I thank you, McKinnon? This is sort of a dream come true for me."You suggest you haven't been writing down every night time for thirty-three nights which you have a residence much like this one?" No, I'm afraid not. So far, it turned into just an idea. But then, mind are things, so right here's my residence!" She twirled round in pride, taking in the kitchen cupboards, new stove and fridge, and the braided rug where her desk and chairs might sit.She stopped short whilst she felt McKinnon's hand on her shoulder."About the thanks, you were going to present me. It's ordinary, but I sense it like a frog. Do I look like a frog to you?"He had turned her to face him, and she or he regarded up at his heat smile."I'm catching the flow, McKinnon, and I'm questioning whether I ought to probably go home and now. Besides, you look a piece extra like a wolf than a frog in the intervening time. His hand turned still on her shoulder, and he lifted her chin along with his palms. Tipping her face up, he bent over and kissed her lightly on the lips. Never a wolf with you, Little Witch. I simply desired to see if the truth got here near to the dream. That little pattern advised me all I desired to understand."

Stepping back, he said depend-of-factly, "Time to go, I bet." Charly changed into still status, rooted to the spot. The idea had crossed her thoughts inside the past few days that if she and McKinnon continued to look at every other, at some point he might try to kiss her. She just wasn't organized for it. Grinning at her, he said, "Coming, Charly?" Moving in the direction of the door, she blushed and spoke back, "Coming, McKinnon." Saturday exceeded like a whirlwind as she packed all of her things, chattered with no end in sight to her mother about her new house, and watched boxes pile up close to the door, ready for moving. Her mom had a hide-a-bed sofa and chair for her den, and fixtures for her second bedroom. Charly had additionally organized for a smartphone to be mounted on Friday. She would have to buy office and dwelling room fixtures, but it would supply her with an awesome excuse to go to auction sales at the weekend.McKinnon showed up together with his truck just after lunch on Sunday and they quickly had it loaded. Her dad and mom followed in their car and the afternoon sped by way of as they organized furnishings and unpacked packing containers. Charly turned aware that McKinnon had had someone come in and clean the residence very well the day before this. It had been musty the day before, however, now it sparkled and smelled find it irresistible has been properly aired.It becomes overdue after they complete, and Charly becomes surprised when McKinnon generalizes her mother's invitation to dine with them. The distance wasn't far and he or she knew this thrilled her parents. They had ignored her in the course of her five years of faculty in Western Ontario and have been glad that she turned once closer to home.She became curious to see if McKinnon might mention something about metaphysics to her dad and mom, however, he kept the communication firmly on farming and she or he guessed that he wasn't but snug discussing it with anyone but herself. Well, Mom, I hate to break this up, however, I've got paintings tomorrow, so I'd higher get domestic." She laughed, and then delivered, "It appears funny to be announcing that, however frankly, I can not wait to get back and spot my residence again."Her dad came over and handed her an envelope. "You can open this when you get there, Charly. It's a little something in the birthday party of your new task." He put his arm around her and hugged her. "Don't neglect to return and go to."Thanks, Dad. I won't."McKinnon accompanied her home in his truck and went inner together with her. "So you think you may stay luckily for your new surroundings?"Oh, McKinnon, do you even need to ask? How ought anyone no longer be satisfied right here?" As an afterthought, she asked, "Would you like a coffee? I think I have all of the requirements."Okay. But I have to test on something downstairs. I'll try this now." When the coffee turned into prepared, McKinnon nonetheless hadn't arisen. Setting up a tray, she decided to take it down, because this is wherein the couch becomes.As quickly as she opened the door to the basement, she could listen to the snapping of the logs in the fireplace and knew he had made her a fireplace."I was given the sensation you were a fire individual, too, Charly." McKinnon became kneeling on the rug by the fire, his denim outlining his muscular body. The sleeves of his crimson wool sweater had been driven above the elbow and he regarded pretty at domestic.Setting the tray down, she smiled at him. "You are proper, McKinnon. I'm very much a fireplace character. In truth, I can also install my office down here, so I can paintings by way of the fireplace."Well, there are masses of wooden piled by way of the fence out again. Help yourself. Oh, my God, McKinnon!" Clapping her give up her mouth, Charly dropped directly to the sofa."What's the matter?" He got here over and sat beside her, alarmed at her pallor."I simply realized I never asked you what the rent change into going to be. How tons, McKinnon? I've been given to find out earlier than I get any extra cushy. I can not consider I did this!" Don't scare me like that, Charly. I concept something turned into sincerely wrong!" Relaxing, he stretched out his legs and positioned his arm alongside the return of the couch in the back of her head."How an awful lot, McKinnon?" Of all the matters she had completed in her existence, this become the craziest.The amount he named became so ridiculously low, that she wasn't positive she had heard correctly. "But I paid almost two times that much for a - bedroom condo inside the metropolis."Forget it, Charly - give up on the debate. Where's that coffee?"Passing him his cup, she settled down beside him, only to feel the letter her Dad had given her crinkling in her pocket. She pulled it out and tore it open. After scanning it, she became in tremendous pleasure to McKinnon. "Do you accept as true with this, McKinnon? He's paid off all of my pupil loans and written off the loan he gave for my SUV. He says if I have been a spoiled brat, he would not have achieved it. He additionally says he would not want the money, so I may as properly have the usage of some of it now, as opposed to ready till he dies. What a man!"Sipping her coffee, she put the cup down and started speaking again.

"Do you realize what this means, McKinnon? I should buy this region as soon as you sever..."Shut up, Charly. You speak an excessive amount of." And all of sudden she changed into in his fingers, his espresso-scented lips corporation and warm on hers.

# CHAPTER FIVE

Tucking her in near his aspect, under his arm, McKinnon drove the hair back from her face. Now tell me how this thirty-three-day element works."Charly had barely caught her breath from the kiss. It was extraordinarily great and pretty sudden. He was a correct kisser - touchy, sensuous and mild all at once. Jerking herself lower back to his query, she speedy assembled her mind."As I recognize it, we're composed of three major parts - conscious, subconscious, and superconscious." She looked up from the hearth into his face, the brown eyes fixed gradually and attentively on her. She referred to idly how lengthy his lashes have been, the slight curl to them. "Carry on. You're doing great. Sounds like basic psychology." When you first nod off, your aware thoughts need to rest, so it steps apart and your unconscious, which doesn't need relaxation or sleep, starts to take over. It critiques the past forty-eight hours and the approaching forty-eight hours, makes a decision if modifications have to be made, what errors have been made that should be corrected, and what's required for tomorrow or. If you bear in mind and examine your dreams, you'll be given directly from your subconscious and superconscious, so one can assist you in your day-by-day dwelling. The unconscious and superconscious are in no way wrong, but they should send messages in symbols so that the aware thoughts disregard it, as it doesn't recognize it, and consequently can't intervene."McKinnon had picked up her left hand and changed into idly gambling along with her Grandmother's ring. She observed she enjoyed the warm temperature of his hands touching her skin."Are you still with me?"Sure am. But where does the superconscious and the thirty-three days are available?"The superconscious is your highest self and retains the memory of what it became you wanted to work on for soul improvement in this lifetime. It critiques your moves and selections and sends messages via profound desires that occur within the deep sleep phase. These desires generally are so different from the average goals that they make a particular influence on you. Often they instruct you to do something you commonly wouldn't don't forget. But don't forget, it's miles by no means wrong. And it's miles in settlement together with your unconscious while it offers you guidelines, so the choice was genuinely yours, although you were blind to making it. You nonetheless following me?"What about the thirty-three days?"Thirty-three days is the normal human cycle. It takes thirty-three days from the inception of thought to a completed selection - a form of like programming yourself. But a good way to convert a notion into truth, there ought to be an agreement at any respect three levels. Since your conscious thoughts want to maintain manipulation, you need to trick them. Thus, the thirty-three-day cycle of writing down something it's far you want. The act of writing it passes it immediately on your unconscious and it can get on with identifying how it's far to be carried out. "Now for the most vital component - the statement I informed you to apply earlier.

If you do not write first that your aware thoughts accept the truth that you desire and deserve something it's far you want, it will throw up all kinds of roadblocks and excuses as to why you shouldn't have it. It additionally on occasion feels that you are not worthy, in particular, if you are requesting wealth and success. So you have to trick it. This is all related to the Universal Law of Attraction as properly – what you recognize on is what you get."And assume I write down that I made love to you?"You can make affirmations related to different people if you like, however, the crucial aspect is your cause. You have to additionally recognize that it isn't viable to make a person else do something they don't want to do. If we had been both in agreement in any respect three ranges of our being, it might in all likelihood take vicinity. But that entails any other whole location of idea and it's getting overdue. I in reality do need to paintings the next day."Okay, correct Little Witch. I'll allow you to get away with an evasive answer this time, however, we'll speak it further later. And it is a promise." He stood slowly, unwinding his period and stretching. She felt a very small status beside him.With McKinnon's departure, the residence appeared unexpectedly extraordinarily empty. With no dwelling room furnishings to absorb the sound, her footsteps echoed as she walked down the hardwood hall floor to her bedroom.Stripping down, she curled her toes within the deep pile of the carpet, enjoying the sensuous feeling of freedom that observed the expertise that she become by myself, absolutely, and could do as she pleased. Her resorts at some point of her pupil days had always been shared and there just wasn't an equal experience of freedom within the town.Smiling and buzzing softly, she went into the shower, nevertheless naked and feeling sinfully unfastened. The water was warm, cascading down over her shoulders, breasts, and hips. She is comfortable under the soothing spray, giving herself as much as the in simple terms physical sensations. Dried and powdered, she once more went naked out of the restroom, across the kitchen, and down to the fireplace to check on it earlier than retiring. The logs had been nonetheless smoldering and throwing warmth out into the room, and he or she stood soaking it into her pores and skin, the glowing heat on her body.Twirling around on her feet, she become once more buzzing as she climbed upstairs and went to the mattress. She slid in underneath the covers, enjoying the texture of the sheets sliding over her pores and skin, slightly cool, the load of the blanket promising warmth inside minutes. As she nestled down and started out slipping into sleep, her frame once more started to tingle with sexual arousal, and she or he knew right away it was coming from McKinnon. Lying nevertheless, she attempted to block it out, however, the feelings had been too sturdy. Her breasts had been throbbing and aching, her legs were becoming susceptible. Her reactions had been so strong that she knew she might be picking up specifics from him very soon if she failed to prevent him. Short of phoning him, there has been little she ought to do except...Sitting up, yoga-like, she did her deep respiratory and cleared her mind after which conjured up his photograph. When it changed into clear, she mentally took his face between her palms and started out kissing him - eyelids, eyebrows, brow, cheeks, chin, earlobes, and in the end his mouth. She concentrated all of her mental electricity on the sensations he could revel in as her lips touched his, just a feather caress first, while her fingers pushed into his hair and exerted just enough stress on his head to preserve it right where she wanted it.She ought to sense the exhilaration construct in his body as she imagined her tongue, warm and wet, going for walks over his lips, lightly prying them open, touching his tooth. She may want to almost hear him gasp, as she slipped her tongue into his mouth to find his, kissing him with a slowly constructing ardor that speedily brought him from passivity to energetic participation. It was at that moment that she suddenly realized McKinnon had somehow joined her in her delusion and in preference to being acted upon, become performing. He becomes transmitting just as powerfully as she becomes and she may want to no longer inform which mind were hers and which his. Nor ought to she shut him out. She changed into stuck and he or she had to participate till he will in any other case.Falling back onto her pillow, she determined that her palms have been clasping her breasts tightly as her mind played scene after scene of flesh in opposition to flesh, breasts in opposition to the hair-roughened chest, tender white thighs against darkish muscular ones, feet entwined, feet curling and caressing in music with tongue and lips. She could experience him kissing her body, inch through trembling inch, the heat building, blood racing, and found out there had been tears in her eyes as it becomes just not sufficient. Nonetheless, he would not permit her to pass. As she lay pissed off and exhausted, she had to well know the fact that McKinnon had shown her very virtually that he became psychically advanced in each way. It apprehensive her, because her very own psychic energy had continually been a fact, shared simplest along with her parents and absolutely below her manipulation. She had lost that manage now and she or he did not like the sensation. The phone with the aid of the mattress rang, startling her so much that she sat bolt upright, then grabbed the receiver. "Hello?" "Welcome domestic, Little Witch. Sleep properly and sweet desires." Click. The connection changed into broken. As she thoughtfully replaced the receiver, she should listen to echoes of the humor in his voice. So, he found it amusing, did he? But despite it all, she slept soundly. As the days, then the weeks, exceeded, she changed into busier than she had ever been earlier in her existence. She did not see McKinnon, and her delusion wasn't repeated, though it turned into in no way very a ways from her mind. Sometimes whilst she changed into a settled-in mattress, she became tempted to send a few electricity to McKinnon, however, the knowledge of his superior energy held her back. She couldn't manage her desires while she changed into asleep, though, and many mornings she would awaken, aware of having had particularly erotic dreams and that McKinnon turned into there together with her. She had studied astral projection and knew it was feasible to proportion desires, however, didn't want to discover it similarly simply now. As the time exceeded, the climate warmed up, leaves came out complete, and vegetation bloomed and died, to get replaced by different, later plant life. Charly turned overjoyed to find a lot of blooms acting and disappearing in her flowerbeds. She spent hours digging around them, pruning shrubs, and setting out some tomato plant life amongst the plants. Today turned into Friday, the cease of June and he or she was going to check out McKinnon's farm. Would he be there? Had he set out his file on purpose? Had someone else set it out? Maybe he did not even recognize she was coming over.She had taken unique care together with her appearance this morning. Her western boots have been sparkling with polish, her jumpsuit changed into pressed with knife-blade sharpness, and her hair has been braided and coiled in a coronet. She had determined to go away from McKinnon's farm until last, just in case he wanted to spend some time with her. It had at a loss for words substantially that he had now not attempted to see her seeing that she had moved into his house. They had turned out to be so close in this type of brief time, like very antique friends, and she simply could not recognize his persevering with silence.

McKinnon had the top reason for his distance from her. He was inside the feed mill at some point waiting on an order to be crammed when Joe Corrigan, a fellow director, and not one in every one of his favorite people, got here up to him."I hear you have our little Inspector tucked away in a nest inside U. S. A.. Cozy. Following your spouse's footsteps, are you?"As his face became beet purple, McKinnon's fist bunched up and his body coiled like an overdrawn bowstring. Struggling to manage, he just muttered, "I'm not even going to dignify that observation with an answer. But I will inform you of this. If I listen you've repeated it everywhere, I'll flatten you. Got that?"Turning on his heel, he stalked out of the mill and roared off in his truck, his order forgotten.

When McKinnon's housekeeper spoke back the door numerous hours later, Charly become dismayed to locate that he turned into in Toronto and wasn't anticipated domestic until tons later in the nighttime. She was so positive she could see him. Hiding her sadness, she went out and started her inspection of the barns and outbuildings. He had a nice run business and the requirements of maintenance have been high, so she did not certainly count on him to discover whatever to document. In reality, she became thinking about why they'd even positioned the document out. As she was about to depart the straw mow, she heard the distinct but susceptible mewling of very young kittens. Memories of searching them out in her father's barn got here flooding lower back, and she set her clipboard and camera to one side, after which began transferring quietly toward the sound.It simplest took her a second, due to the fact mamma cat had heard them as properly and become on her manner to feed them. Charly couldn't face up to taking them from their hiding location and cuddling them for a few moments. One especially caught her fancy. He became all black, a little larger than the relaxation, and plenty more competitive."So, little Bagheera, you're going to be king of the jungle, are you?" He seemed up at her with big, liquid eyes, blinking, however, mendacity was still in her hand. "Tell me, where's McKinnon? Why hasn't he called me? I idea perhaps we might be friends, however, it looks as if I turned into very wrong. I suppose socializing with a worker is simply as a lot a no-no here as it'd be in a large city workplace. But damn it, I enjoy speaking to him."The kitten became squirming to get his lunch, so she positioned him down beside his mother, and laughed when he tried to stroll and toppled over in the straw. He turned into quickly eagerly feeding together with his siblings."Bye, little Bagheera. Grow strong and capture masses of mice." She spoke softly as she accrued up her matters and went out into the sunshine. She did not pay attention to the footsteps pause at the ways give up of the barn, nor see the tall figure standing so quietly, simply listening.Restlessness plagued her later that nighttime as she attempted to find something to do. Staying in on Friday nights hadn't her before, but tonight changed into someway exceptional, probable because she had constructed up her hopes of seeing McKinnon, handiest to be disillusioned. Driven with excess strength and no outlet, she sooner or later pulled on some old types of denim and a plaid shirt, braided her hair, and took gardening equipment out to the flowerbeds.She become attacking the weeds with unaccustomed energy when she heard an automobile. As she rounded the corner of the house, she stopped in mid-stride. McKinnon becomes getting out of his black Cadillac."Hi Witch. What's new?"Warily, she looked at him. He changed into acting as though they had just parted a few hours ago, in place of several weeks."Not tons. To what do I owe the delight of your agency?"Becoming unexpectedly extreme, he stated, "I desired to speak to you. I hope I haven't come at a bad time."Oh, very terrible, McKinnon. I'm busy unique the mayor and his spouse for tea. Can't you tell by using my attire?" She grinned at him as she pulled off her grubby gloves. "Come on in."Since McKinnon had remaining been within the residence, Charly had managed to finish furnishing it. She presented him with a seat inside the living room whilst she cleaned up, and she was puzzled as she did so what it can be that he wanted to talk about. She wasn't long locating out. He changed into pacing around the room whilst she came back and her defenses rose due to the fact she should sense that it wasn't going to be good news."Something's wrong, isn't it, McKinnon?"Yes, Charly, something's wrong. I'm now not sure I can talk approximately this without blowing up."I suppose you had better simply inform me what it's far. I'll make a few coffees whilst you get your thoughts together." Was he going to tell her she turned into the fire? Or that he had offered the assets and he or she needed to get out of the residence? Filling cups, she carried them out to the residing room."Is it something I've executed, McKinnon? You're scowling like a bear with a thorn in his paw."God, no Charly. It surely hasn't whatever to do with you, besides that, you happen to be living in my residence." He sat down and picked up his coffee, staring blankly out the window."Come on, T. G., tell me. I can't stand the suspense. Just tell me what occurred to disappointed you." She sank beside him, wanting to provide consolation however not knowing a way to give it because she failed to know yet what the trouble became."Maybe it truly is a nice way. I'll just inform you what came about and you can surmise the relaxation." "Okay, shoot."Briefly, he mentioned the confrontation inside the feed mill. "So you spot, Charly, this whole situation is not possible."Stunned, she stared at him. "Are you asking me to transport out, McKinnon?" "Good heavens, no. I wouldn't let everybody pressure me right into a decision like that." "Then are you asking me to stop my process?"I don't have the right to do this either. I wouldn't expect you to do it."Then what do you want from me?" Puzzled and careworn, she persevered to stare at him."I do not need anything from you, Charly, besides your understanding. You see, with humans thinking and pronouncing such things as that, we can not see every other socially. I desired you to recognize why you were not listening to me. I simply may not have you exposed to that sort of malicious gossip."For God's sake, McKinnon, the gossip can't harm me, or you either, for that depends. Didn't you listen to whatever I informed you? The only people harmed using that type of issue are the originators of the thoughts and words. Not us." She positioned her cup cautiously on the coffee desk. "Never us."I recognize that on one level, Charly, but on any other, I simply see purple and need to punch someone out, and that is damaging to my soul, trust me. Especially if I wallop my co-director in a public region." He set his cup beside hers and rose to begin pacing again. "It's simply little need, Charly. We had something really special growing between us, however, I might not let them smash it with their malicious gossip. So it has to be over earlier than it even has a danger to start."There's not anything I can say to exchange your mind?"Nothing. I've been thinking about it for hours and I can't see any other solution. I need to stay to this point far away from here and from you so no one can point a finger at both folks. It would provide positive people a good opportunity to mention you should in no way have been hired, if they may even hint that we were having an affair. And this is a completely small network." "I cannot agree with that is taking place, McKinnon. I feel like I'm dropping my great buddy. Would you keep me for a minute?" She had risen and stood watching him, her emotions obvious in her tear-filled eyes.Crossing the gap that separated them, he accumulated her into his hands, wrapping them tightly around her and holding her close in opposition to him. He dropped his head and rested his cheek on her hair. They stood silently for long moments. Charly drew consolation from the warm temperature of his arms and frame. It felt so right to be near him. How ought people make it into something unsightly? She didn't need their friendship to end now. There became so much more she desired to know approximately him, so many things yet to discover.For only a moment, she considered the opportunity of seducing him and making him need her a lot he would not have the ability to mention no, but only for a second. It would be clean enough. Just raise her head, contact her lips to his and repeat the fantasy they'd shared formerly. Her thoughts started out playing it back as she stood soaking in the warmth and fragrance and feel of him. Suddenly she felt him shudder and knew instinctively he had picked up her thoughts. Trying to blank her thoughts, she moved to step lower back from the circle of his hands, however as she lifted her head from his chest, his lips moved over hers and settled firmly on them, as if coming home.Now the fantasy has become three-dimensional truth, with brought bonuses. She should contact him as he became touching her, experience the thick softness of his hair as her hands slipped into it, since the acceleration of his pulse, and sense the throb of his heartbeat after hers. She should pay attention to his respiration quicken because the kiss deepened and she or he sensed that he was unexpectedly achieving his limits of management.Her frame become responding as it had in her delusion, giving us a great deal as she turned into taking, encouraging him to respond to her needs, with the aid of a little strain here, a subtle motion there, all carried out unconsciously and clearly. As his arms slipped from her face down to her rib cage, his palms just beneath her breasts, she arched her body nearer, his arousal alive and demanding in opposition to her. Her palms slid down over his shoulders to pull him even closer as the kiss they had been sharing lifted them to heights simplest hinted at in their fantasies. But his palms had barely closed over her breasts to inflame them along with his heat, while he pushed himself far from her, holding his hands up as though to ward her off."Stop me now, Charly, please!" His voice become anguished as he turned his back to her."I cannot prevent myself, McKinnon. I don't need to. So if you want to stop this, you would higher go away now." Tears had been falling, but she tried to preserve them out of her voice."Charly...""Go, McKinnon. For God's sake, simply move." She becomes standing together with her palms clasped tightly around her middle, protecting her ache. She watched as he unclenched his fists and strode unexpectedly out of the house without a backward look. She heard the engine revving and the tires tearing into the gravel as he spun out of the driveway. She felt a high-quality vacancy invading her soul because the loneliness of the future stretched before her. No more deep voice calling her `Little Witch'. No greater discussions about metaphysics, but most of all, no more laughing and deepening comradeship with her pal.

# CHAPTER SIX

It had been years because Charly had cried herself to sleep, so tonight she made up for a misplaced time. She knew all the arguments about expert ethics, getting involved with superiors, and behaving in a way that would purpose people to speak. It became vital that she keeps a terrific picture in the community if she wished to keep the honor of the clients in addition to the directors and group of workers. If only his spouse had behaved extraordinarily. But knowing all of the reasons why they could not be collectively didn't make the pain any less. For some time she mulled over the opportunity of resigning and taking some other job, but in which? There wasn't some other insurance enterprise for miles, or even if McKinnon did need to peer her again, she could be too a long way away. Maybe he ought to resign as a director. She was certain from what she had visible of his farm, that he failed to want the director's fees. But then, that wouldn't be a truthful answer to both. She fell into an exhausted sleep, only to wake a couple of hours later, tears streaming from her eyes and a feeling of dread that she could not shake. She got up and wandered around for some time, made a cup of mint tea and drank it, then sat in the darkened living room and tortured herself with recollections of the closing scene with him. Her mind replayed all of it, from his first phrases to her remaining. She relived all of the feelings and feelings once more, but the unhappiness in her took away all the joy she had felt in his arms. Her soul becomes crying out for its mate with an intensity of feeling she had by no means earlier than experienced. It changed into a very long night. Somehow, Charly managed to hold on together with her activity. She gave it all of her attention, writing meticulous reviews, making very targeted inspections, updating photos that truly did not want it, and putting in a lot longer hours than was expected of her. When the personnel commenced to touch upon her apparent weight reduction, and the long hours she became working, hinting that perhaps she was working too difficult, she attempted to stay out of the workplace as a great deal as possible so that they wouldn't know what she turned into doing. She regarded up vintage pals, however, they lost hobby in her when she become unable to give them her complete attention. Her maximum glad times were those spent on my own together with her flowerbeds, or taking walks out thru the woods across the road. Then one morning she awakened feeling nauseated and headachy. She decided it become a bout of summer flu, so took some Vitamin C and carried on. As the day stepped forward, so did her feelings of soreness. By past due afternoon, she had extreme cramps in her stomach and had to cut her final inspection brief. She knew she became fevered by the time she was given a home and the pain had accelerated a lot, she commenced to panic. It couldn't be just flu. It changed into too intense for that. Picking up the telephone, she referred to as her dad and mom, best remembering after the fifteenth ring that they'd gone up north for a month of fishing. It turned into about a half of-hour drive to the health center and she or he knew she wanted clinical interest. Gathering up her handbag and keys, she went again out to the auto and drove to Belleville.

McKinnon had just sat right down to an overdue dinner while he doubled over with severe stomach cramps. He had felt quality until the simplest moments before. Clutching his belly, he went into his bedroom and fell to the bed, knees drawn up to his chest. He stayed like that for an hour, whilst the pain eventually eased and he turned into able to stand upright with little discomfort. Assuming it turned into something he had eaten, he went about his commercial enterprise. It wasn't until two weeks later when he was in the workplace for their month-to-month meeting, that the supervisor asked him how his new tenant was."What do you mean?"I imply Charly. How is she?" The supervisor turned into searching at him surprisingly. "Is something incorrect along with her?" McKinnon was all at once very attentive."You need to understand. She's living in your house. She had her appendix out weeks in the past. Where have you ever been?"I do not see her if that is what you mean. She rents my house and that is it. I didn't realize something about it. I surprise where she is now?"I heard she went to her uncle's from the medical institution. Her dad and mom are away. She had a nurse call in the next day to inform us she would not be again for a minimum of four weeks. How approximately doing a little inspection for us?"Sure. Anytime." McKinnon wasn't certainly paying attention. He has to have known. To assume she had to go through that without even a card from him! She ought to assume he became a brute. The meeting dragged on forever, it seemed to him. He could not wait to break out from what was regarded as very petty issues. His mind was miles away but nobody seemed to observe. Finally, he became capable of making his excuses and hurrying to his automobile. The others were meeting at the president's house as they from time to time did, however, he just pleaded a prior engagement and sped to the florist, hoping the store wouldn't be closed. Choosing a huge bunch of crimson carnations and potted ivy, he positioned them in the automobile, then went into the closest branch save and picked out the softest, maximum loveable teddy bear he ought to find. A forestall at the grocery shop for a few blended kinds of cheese and fruit, and then an aspect journey into a bookstore simply as the girl become about to shut up, and his purchases had been entire. Except for one aspect. He stepped right into a cellphone sales space, dialed her range, and hung up as quickly as she replied. Had she still been staying together with her uncle, he might have had a brilliant time explaining his purchases to his housekeeper. One more journey into the Chinese eating place to the region an order for take-out, and his plans have been entire. Except for some wine. But the store was already closed. Damn!What if she had already eaten? What if she went out someplace earlier than he got there? What if she didn't want to look at him? He attempted to live calm as he drove into her yard and gathered up his purchases. With arms full, he needed to push the doorbell together with his elbow. It regarded to take all the time before she opened the door. And all of sudden the effort became worthwhile. His doubts all vanished as he noticed her face light up like a candle

Charly replaced the receiver thoughtfully. Who would call and then cling up when she answered? Shrugging her shoulders, she assumed it became someone who had reached an incorrect range and went returned to the sofa and her e-book. She was reading continuously seeing that she was back domestic, except for each day stroll, as ordered by the medical doctor. She was considering McKinnon too. It had been so difficult inside the health facility with no one but her aunt and uncle to visit. She had refused to allow them to name her dad and mom, due to the fact she knew they had been looking ahead to the trip. There turned into not anything they may do for her anyway.Day after day she lay in the hospital thinking if McKinnon could be available to peer her. Day after day handed without a sign of him. And as soon as she become cellular, she stood by the phone often, speaking herself out of calling him. Now the worst changed over. She was lower back in her little residence, her fitness was on the mend, and she or he had survived without him.Settling back off, she lost herself all over again in her e-book, promising to make something to devour after the subsequent bankruptcy.The doorbell startled her into jumping up, swearing as the muscle tissues in her stomach protested. She made her way extra slowly to the door, hoping it wasn't all people important. She had all started wearing a cushy multi-colored caftan due to the fact her surgery and her hair was swinging around her shoulders, unfastened. Her toes were bare. Pulling the door open, she gasped, after which smiled widely. "McKinnon. Hi! Come on in." Stepping aside, she held the door as he struggled to the table, trying no longer to drop anything.Shoving the plants at her, he requested all of sudden, "Charly, why the hell didn't you name me? Never mind. I shouldn't even ask." Groaning, he pulled her into his hands, his mouth gentle and warm on hers. Kissing her very well, he stepped again and allow her to move."Better placed than vegetation in the water. I think perhaps we overwhelmed them a little." Sheepishly, he attempted to straighten them."We? What do you imply we, McKinnon?" Laughing, she went out to the kitchen and stuffed a vase. She had a problem retaining her emotions below manage, she was so satisfied to see him. When she returned, McKinnon turned into standing again, the teddy undergo held in his arms, a silly grin on his face. "I think I went a touch crazy after I located out what you have been through, Charly. I desire a person who had advised me when it happened. Nothing would have stored me away." He walked in the direction of her, protecting the teddy undergo. "This is for you. I'm not even positive why I bought it. It just regarded the factor to do at the time."It turned into precisely the right issue to do. I've been collecting crammed bears for years. I have containers of them in my mom's basement. Maybe I'll convey them over and deliver them a place to take a seat inside the spare room. After all, this guy would probably revel in the business enterprise." Charly knew she turned into babbling again but couldn't help it. He changed into right here with her at ultimate."Come and sit down, Witch. I need to hear all about it. Was it without a doubt terrible? If the jolt I had become any indication, you certainly didn't have plenty amusing." And he advised her about being doubled up with ache the day of her surgical treatment."Are you going to enter labor when I have a toddler, too, McKinnon?" She teased him."I positive could if it was my toddler. Oh, Charly, why did you have to carry up that challenge? I can't keep my thoughts off of creating love with you as it is. I like your get dressed, by way of the manner." He became smiling at her, his legs stretched out in front of him, fingers across the lower back of the sofa behind her. One hand becomes gambling idly along with her hair, although she concept he become ignorant of it. "How about a few Chinese meals? Or have you eaten?" He knew they needed to get concerned about something immediately or he would take her in his hands and neglect his better judgment. Chatting as she labored, putting in plates and cutlery, Charly advised him about her medical institution stay, her restoration, and she enforced retirement. "I hope the organization isn't always mad at me for goofing off so soon after being employed."Of course no longer. Having emergency surgery isn't always goofing off. How did you get to the clinic, by the way? I heard your mother and father had been away while it befell."They're now not returned yet. I drove myself to the clinic. It wasn't too comfortable, but I made it."Damn it, Charly! Haven't you got any feel? Don't you realize your appendix ought to have ruptured? Why did not you call me?"She had visible McKinnon withdrawn, sarcastic, passionate, funny, and detached. But she hadn't seen him angry, until now. And he becomes furious. It was a pleasant feeling, to recognize that he cared a lot."But it didn't, so don't have a coronary over it, McKinnon. I'm exceptional, you're pleasant, the teddy bear is best, we are all fine, so loosen up and devour." She slapped a plate down in front of him none too gently and surpassed him with the Soya sauce.Silence reigned for numerous moments, till Charly should stand it not. "For heaven's sake, McKinnon, loosen up. Stop sulking. We haven't seen every different for eons and we're preventing it. I can't stand it!"I'm no longer sulking, for your information. I simply don't want to see people take useless dangers. And you probably did. I idea you promised to call me if you had any problems."Work troubles, McKinnon. And that was before we decided now not to peer each other anymore. Remember?"Don't remind me. Oh, hell, permit's just forget it and enjoy the time we've got."They controlled to overlook their variations for the remainder of a very quality night. They also stayed away from any discussion in their selection not to peer every other. Charly became content material to revel in his company for so long as he stayed along with her."Would you do me a favor, Charly?" McKinnon changed into sitting across from her, downstairs via the hearth, and grinning at her with an almost sheepish appearance. She questioned what became coming subsequent."If I'm able, sure. What would you want?"I've been remembering and writing down a number of my desires however I have no idea how to research them. If I ship a few over, could you've got a examine them and notice what you make of them?"Are you certain you need me to peer them, McKinnon? Dreams are about as non-public as you could get."There's no one else I'd agree with them with. Besides, I realize you will be tactful. After all, you are an awesome witch, proper?" "Right. Okay, ship them over and I'll do what I can. Some symbols are quite popular, but others will be specific to you. If you will ruin your goals down into the important elements for me and imply what the various things imply to you, it will make it less difficult to analyze them."Can you give me an instance of what you mean?" McKinnon turned into all seriousness now."Okay. Suppose you dream of cows. Normally they constitute self-indulgence, but since you paint with them all the time, they may truly mean work to you. It's additionally quite crucial that you describe the putting, the people, shades, sports, whether or not you're looking at or participating, how near you're to the motion, the general feeling the dream leaves you with, and any words, names or number that appear. Sort of like doing a homework project."She threw another log on the fire and sat down again."Quite often the messages may be funny. For example, in case you have been to dream of being given a new enamel brush with a small horse head on the bristle end, the message might be that you should watch out for looking like a gift horse in the mouth, likely about dental care. Those are the kinds I like exceptional because I love puzzles."McKinnon turned into giggling, amusement and skepticism both evident in his expression. "Do people in reality dream stuff like that, or are you placing me on?"They without a doubt do. I should even show it to you because it's certainly one of mine. Another time when I asked for a dream to explain a previous dream I could not discern, I dreamed I turned into having my skull measured to peer how thick it become. I woke up guffawing and the relaxation of the dream gave me sufficient clues that I should figure out the first one."Would you show me some of your goals? It sounds like a truthful change to me. Besides, if I examine your dreams together with your interpretations it will assist me to find out how to analyze mine."Maybe I will. I'd want to appearance them over earlier than I give you any of them even though. I even have dreams going as a long way lower back as I can recall, but I didn't always write out interpretations. I commonly examine them on Sundays for the beyond a week to get some concept of what I'm going through in my life, and if there may be anything mainly I must or should not be doing. I'll go through the final week's goals and put interpretations on them, then I'll send them to you.What's your mailing cope with?"She wrote it out on a chunk of paper and tucked it into her pocket. Then she smothered a yawn as she settled extra comfortably in her chair."Oh, Charly, I'm sorry! I failed to recognize it changed into so overdue. You ought to be tired, however, I changed into playing myself a lot I forgot you're nevertheless an invalid." Rising, he walked over to her, and putting his hands on the palms of her chair, leaned over and kissed her gently on the forehead. "I'll see myself out and I'll ship you a few desires first aspect the following day. Sleep nicely and dream properly."Before she ought to rise, he turned into long past up the steps in numerous bounds, and he or she heard the door closing at the back of him. She knew why he hadn't wanted a prolonged goodbye. They were simply too painful.

# CHAPTER SEVEN

Charly found herself re-reading her dreams over the following few days with an exceptional angle. To examine them over become one issue, however, to have McKinnon reading them and knowing what they are supposed to her change into going to be like letting him into her innermost thoughts. But then, he became willing to permit her to see his.She looked after out some of the fines for studying functions, going returned over numerous years. She turned grateful now that she had kept them in loose-leaf shape so that she could be selective. To have him privy to all of them became just too threatening for the moment.She determined herself watching for the mailman on Monday morning and once more on Tuesday. As soon as he pulled far away from the mailbox, she could hurry out to retrieve her mail, hoping for the bundle from McKinnon. She changed into burning with curiosity to see what he had been dreaming.When the package deal did arrive, it came within the nighttime and became tucked in between her front doors. She found it when she went out to check the climate Wednesday morning.Rushing inside, she poured espresso and sat down. With trembling arms, she tore open the massive manila envelope and pulled out the typewritten sheets of paper.Clipped to the top of the first page turned into a note, scrawled in his specific, corporation handwriting."Here they're. This is going again to the first one I remember after our communication on the concern and consists of every dream I've had when you consider that. Will hold on to writing. Happy translating! T.G."Charly had mailed some of hers off to him and expected that he would have obtained them already. Just understanding that he could be analyzing them made her experience very near him.She settled down greater with ease and started out scanning the pages in the front of her, images and sensations flooding via her as she allowed herself to flow along with his dreams. A very strong sense of his character started out coming thru to her and she or he examine quickly to the ultimate web page. Closing her eyes, she dropped her head back against the sofa and let the emotions waft for some moments. Uppermost become a feeling of satisfaction on the high quality of the self-cognizance evident in his goals, and the encouragement he was being given to holding. She roused herself and started writing rapidly, giving a brief outline of the overall subject matter of his dreams, then a more specific translation of a number of the symbols.Time passed, with best the sound of the pen in opposition to the paper and the occasional rustle as she started a sparkling sheet. When she subsequently ran out of phrases, she arched her back and rubbed the nape of her neck. With a clean coffee beside her, she began re-studying what she had written, looking to see it via his eyes, instead of her very own, wondering if it might make an experience for him. With little or no modification, she decided it was entire, and went into her workplace to procedure it on her pc.The pc system became her deal with once the truth that she was completely debt-unfastened had registered. She had taken into consideration the opportunity of compiling all of her desires right into a magazine, and the concept commenced to take preserve, with McKinnon's hobby within the difficulty.A sample developed over the subsequent weeks, one which she located immensely pleasurable. Her days revolved around reviewing her dreams in addition to his, and the highlight of her days changed into the retrieval of the fats applications from the mailbox, and her enjoyment in learning him thoroughly. He had begun slipping little personal notes into every package deal and he or she was replying with her personal, so she becomes able to preserve abreast of what became happening in his existence, on all ranges. As the weeks surpassed, she explained to him the means of his dreams, but she also took the time to train him on how to interpret them on his personal, suggesting that he get a few file playing cards and begin his very own non-public dream dictionary. She defined that the identical symbols could start to seem repetitive and whilst he had them documented, he could soon analyze what they intended for him. She also advised him that a diary of everyday occasions and happenings could be of assistance as properly so that he should relate dreams to real stories. And a way to have a look at different people in his desires and, taking the primary robust function that got here to thoughts approximately them, apply it to his scenario." The language of dreams is one of the oldest on the planet, and needs to be found out like every overseas language," she wrote one day, in solution to his query about why she become personalizing everything. "Your unconscious thoughts look for something in image form so that it will get a message across. You need to learn how to translate those snapshots into words. Remember that your dreams, for the most part, are approximately you and for you. That's why they may be personalized."It became pretty a while earlier than he despatched a dream which contained a story approximately his making like to any other girl, and she or he smiled to herself as she interpreted it for him, understanding that he had probably had more than one, but hadn't pretty had the braveness to send them to her."This dream symbolizes the combination of the alternative components of your self - the solidarity forming with your subconscious and superconscious minds, and the female factors of your character. It has not anything to do with intercourse. However, ought to your dream of rabbits..."Then another day whilst his dream said truly, `Dreamed of a group of celery and a few lettuces', she wrote again immediately, `Eat greater clean vegetables! If you notice meals this is black or has an X on them, it way that you should keep away from them. Chalk up another one to your appropriate old subconscious. He's trying to get your body into a better bodily situation, so pay interest."As his dreams commenced to reveal greater depth, and logos indicating cleaning with greater frequency, she instructed him to be organized for long-forgotten reminiscences to start surfacing.`The symbols of washing, doing laundry, and tub towels, are a way of telling you that you are getting rid of quite a few `rubbish' which you've been carrying around for your unconscious. If you locate yourself becoming very quiet inner a few days, simply burst off with the aid of yourself and loosen up. A reminiscence will floor and alongside it'll come a higher understanding of it.Recognize it and let it move. Each time this occurs, you may locate yourself starting to feel lighter, even though that isn't always clearly an appropriate period.

Another of these things that would be better described with symbols!"There have been dreams that she could not interpret and she advised him to come back to them in numerous weeks, perhaps even months, due to the fact they were possibly approximately future events and would make feel in a while. And she told him what it meant when he dreamed of an explosion in which he was killed. 'This does now not mean to write down out your will and buy a coffin. It's a way that there's a major trade about to take region within you.Congratulations! Your progress is awesome!"She nevertheless took exceptional care and pride in her process, managing problems that came up with professionalism that amazed her at instances. She become privy to a newfound peace within herself and decided that it got here from the closeness she changed into sharing with McKinnon thru their dreams. And she was usually aware of how her feelings for him have been turning deeper and stronger because the days, weeks, and months slipped by using. As Christmas approached, she started to pray that they might spend even some hours together. She longed to feel his hands around her once more, his lips on hers. She had kept a damper on all sexual feelings, however, she determined, as she concept of seeing him, they commenced to the floor. Her mind become weaving daydreams of an evening by the hearth shared with him, the exchange of presents, the tree with its decorations sparkling in the firelight, the scent of wood smoke, and the crackle of logs as they burned. Her notion is lengthy and tough approximately what she may want to deliver him for a Christmas present and eventually settled on an e-book that she felt might assist him the maximum.

It become an ebook of dream interpretations that she had located very beneficially while she was first getting to know the manner.She had almost satisfied herself the dream changed into real, whilst it becomes burst like a soap bubble, without any warning. The standard package deal arrived on the Monday morning before Christmas. The note changed into connected to the pinnacle web page, as regular.`My Dear Little Witch:'`I need a lot to spend Christmas with you. You can not realize how a whole lot. But if I have been to spend five minutes with you presently, I wouldn't be capable of going away, and we each recognize that an affair might be disastrous to your reputation. I've determined to take myself off to Australia for a month where I'll visit an uncle and a few cousins I have not seen in approximately ten years.How I desire you have been coming with me.'`I had no intentions of getting non-public, but I discover that the greater I take a look at my desires, and yours, the closer I sense to you. I often have the strong effect that you are considering me and I consider we share many moments without being together. You have ended up very vital to me, as a chum and as a teacher, and as you likely are very well conscious, I don't supply or receive friendship effortlessly.'`I will take you with me after I leave this morning and hold you with me until I go back. I'll omit our shared goals and little notes extra than I can say, but the month will bypass fast and I'll have a huge fats envelope for you after I get it again. Have a very good Christmas and think of me on Christmas morning. Take a stroll inside the snow for me - I'll be playing summer weather `down below.It turned into actually signed, `Love, T. G.' and she realized she became crying as she folded the paper and again it to the envelope.Somehow, she made it via the month. Since her heart scene of Christmas had evaporated, she genuinely wrapped the ebook and mailed it to him, knowing he wouldn't get hold of it until he lower back. She half of-hoped he might smartphone on Christmas Eve or perhaps New Year, but each holiday exceeded silently and she or he tried to place on a shiny face for her dad and mom. Never had she experienced such devastating loneliness. The hours and days dragged by means and she or he relived their whole courting from starting to quit, questioning what future they had, searching for an option to their situation, for she knew he wasn't going to see her so long as she becomes running for the agency.Her very own desires started out containing chase scenes and she or he realized she was being `chased' through her person - doubts, and fears for the future of their friendship. She frequently wakened with tear-stained cheeks, however, no reminiscence of getting been crying.The week before McKinnon changed into the due back, the manager called her into his workplace when she went in to select up some documents."You've been with us for quite some time and we're very pleased with your performance. How approximately a reward? There's an Insurance Convention in Toronto on the Sheraton Centre in March and, due to the fact numerous of the audio system could be speaking approximately subjects as a way to be of interest to you, the Directors have authorized me to invite you to join us this twelve months. Your costs will all be paid, of direction, and the conference lasts for three days. What approximately is it? Shall I sign up for you?"Charly stood observing him. Although well conscious that there had been conventions for twelve months, one for the

Presidents and Managers and one for the full Board of Directors, it had in no way happened to her that she is probably protected. Immediately her mind flipped to McKinnon. If she went, could he stay home? If she did not go, might he wonder why? If they each went..."Can I think about it for multiple days? You've stuck me by surprise."Only a couple, please. We should allow the resort to recognize how many rooms we require and we like to get them in a block, if viable. Can you let me realize by using the day after the following day? I sense it'd be very beneficial with a view to cross because they typically maintain us published on any new statistics approximately hearth prevention equipment, alarm structures, and other topics that observe in your location of duty."Okay, I'll come up with my decision then." And she walked out to her car, feeling as though the ground had fallen out from below her.The answer got here to her the following morning as she become writing out her goals. It becomes all there for her to peer - the experience, the lectures, and the banquet - properly, nearly all. She did not see McKinnon everywhere inside the desires. So I'll pass. I wager that means he'll be staying domestic. She wasn't sure whether or not she must be pleased or disillusioned, but she advised the manager to e-book her in while she went into the office later in the day.True to his word, McKinnon had a total bundle of desires for her when he lower back. She was disillusioned to locate his word almost impersonal, with most effective a thumbnail sketch of his journey and one small sentence approximately having missed her. She set the dreams apart until the weekend, just not feeling as much as the emotional upheaval of analyzing thru them.She knew now and had acknowledged for some time, that she changed into very an awful lot in love with him. She simply didn't need to well know the reality, because to accomplish that meant that she would have to make a choice approximately it, even supposing that decision become to just accept the fame quo and keep on along with her lifestyle. During the month he changed into away, she had come to realize that she changed geared up to accept any type of dating with him that he might allow her. It amazed her to locate that she was very calm about the reality that she no longer cared what others might reflect on consideration on either of them.As the day of the conference drew closer, she located herself turning excited about it, and frequently requested herself why. She went shopping for a few new garments and chose a get dressed with first-rate take care of the feast that she would be expected to wait for. Right as much as the remaining moment, she believed that McKinnon wasn't going, because he hadn't been in her desires of the conference.The closing minute arrived and he or she all at once realized that dreams did not always inform all. The supervisor had informed her they might be pooling motors for the experience to Toronto to shop for gasoline, and she or he changed into meeting the others at the office on Wednesday morning. When she arrived, she discovered them already loading automobiles and wondered whom she could be riding with, but not being concerned."Hi, Charly. I've put you in T. G.'s car if this is ok with you. He appears to be the only one without a full load." She became quick and, for the first time, noticed him. He became standing beside the black Cadillac, tons as he were on that first day that appeared like years in the past - legs crossed on the ankles, palms folded on his chest, and no smile. She looked uncertainly at him, then shrugged and started out unloading her matters from the again of her SUV.He changed without delay at her facet, taking the suitcase and garment bag from her, leaving just her purse for her to hold. He had the trunk loaded and closed in seconds and turned into conserving open the passenger door for her, whilst it dawned on her that the others had driven off and she or he became his only passenger. She did not understand whether to giggle or cry. She simplest knew she wasn't prepared for this.

# CHAPTER EIGHT

It became with a feeling of deja vu that she settled within the seat and became resigned to the two-and-a-half of-hour ride, wondering if he might talk to her, ignore her, tease her, or make love together with her."You seemed a chunk taken aback whilst you found out I became going to the convention, Charly. Why?" He seemed sideways at her as he swung the car out into the visitors."Because you weren't in my dreams, it's why!" She spoke sharply, still unsettled. "I saw the entire conference in a dream weeks ago and you were not there, so I assumed you would not be going."Who was it that advised me once one needs no means to count on anything? I knew we were going collectively earlier than I left for Australia because I also saw the convention and I truly saw you there. Relax, Little Witch. The dream stated we had a first-rate time, so permit's simply experienced ourselves. God best is aware of, we deserve it." The last became uttered underneath his breath, but she caught it and discovered herself smiling.From then on, her mood commenced to improve and he or she started out firing questions at him concerning his vacation in Australia, a place she had always desired to go to. The ride turned over earlier than she realized it and he or she was nonetheless wondering him as they accompanied the bellhop into the foyer and waited for their rooms to be assigned.She barely noticed as he accrued their keys and walked with her to the elevator. He was nonetheless speaking to her about his trip, as they paused for the bellhop to open their doorways and area their luggage internal. But she eventually awoke as much as fact whilst he crossed from his room into hers via the connecting door."Sorry, we c, couldn't get all of the rooms together on your agency, however, we m, managed to preserve all of you near someone else from the organization." The bellhop time-honored the top McKinnon passed him and left.Kicking the door to her room close, McKinnon abruptly reached for her and pulled her into his palms. His mouth closed over hers in a long, slow kiss and she melted against him, relaxing into the haven of his hands. Ending the kiss, he pulled her more tightly towards his chest and just held her silently for a long second. She closed her eyes, savoring closeness, and experience of rightness."I don't know who we must thank for our room association, however, I'm, now not going to impeach it or bitch approximately it." He released her and stepped lower back just as someone knocked at the door of his room. "I'll see you earlier than the banquet tonight." And he becomes through the door.Charly unpacked her things, striking her clothes up within the closet. She knew she didn't have a lecture to attend for multiple hours and he or she also knew that McKinnon could be tied up for the relaxation of the day. She became nevertheless musing over the tenderness of his kiss and the warmth of his embrace. She knew honestly that they might make love earlier than the stop of the convention and she or he became content material to permit it to appear whilst the time was right.She did not think beyond the convention of existence in the County. She just knew she cherished him and became sure he loved her as well. She changed into humming to herself as she finished unpacking and went thankfully to her lecture. She paid close interest to the speaker because she nonetheless had a job to do and he or she become right here at the expense of the employer, so she could fulfill her duties. When the lecture become completed, she hurried as much as the room to see McKinnon, only to find a word as an alternative.`Have to make the rounds of the hospitality suites. See you at the dinner party.'In a manner, she changed into pleased because it supposed that she may want to take her time getting bathed and dressed. She knew a dance accompanied the banquet, however, she failed to fear approximately the seating preparations, the dance, or something else that would transpire. She was content material to let occasions unroll of their manner and time, understanding that it might be right.When she turned dressed and made up and McKinnon nevertheless hadn't back, she waited till it changed into almost time for the dinner party after which went right down to the hall. Each of the ladies become being given a small corsage and she waited in line for hers, searching round now with interest, thinking in which he might be. She was given her meal ticket and knew what table she become assigned, but she had no idea if he would be on the equal one.Her corsage pinned in place, she slowly entered the room, not seeing any of her institutions. She wove her manner thru the tables, studying the numbers as she went, in the end finding hers within the corner near the dais. None of the others had arrived yet, so she treated herself to a front-dealing with a chair. She has become absorbed in analyzing the dresses the other ladies have been carrying. Many of the administrators had brought their better halves with them, even though her agency did not achieve this.She felt a hand choose her shoulder and regarded up to see McKinnon smiling down into her eyes. He pulled out the chair next to her and settled himself close beside her. Like he truly would not supply a rattling what everybody else thinks.His behavior towards her at some stage in dinner and the speeches became friendly, but he kept his feedback popular and covered the others in their conversations as a lot as feasible. When dinner become over, but, he claimed her for the first dance and led her out onto the floor with an arm around her shoulders.Before the dance ended, she knew it was a mistake for them to participate. So a whole lot had passed off between them inside the past few months with no bodily contact that they were attuned to every other to some extent she had by no means experienced before. She knew what he become going to mention earlier than he started it, she knew what he turned into feeling with no phrases being spoken, and she became aware that he wanted her as badly as she wanted him."When this wide variety is over, follow my lead and consider something I say. We ought to get out of right here." As they moved in time to the track, collectively however apart, she pressured herself to the cognizance of the music, the people around them, whatever but his heat and sensuous frame so close to her own. Twice he stepped on her toe and apologized, swearing the second time it passed off.When the track stopped, different couples stayed in place for the following number, but McKinnon advised her quickly off the floor to their table, wherein numerous of the directors have been deep in `Insurance speak' as she referred to it. They seemed up and grinned as

McKinnon said, "I'm taking our inspector out to a movie. She's too young to be cooped up in right here with most of these antique fogies."His voice was mild and his smile was sincere, however, she ought to experience the tension jogging deep internal of him, slightly held in the test. Bidding the others goodnight, she picked up her purse and walked with McKinnon to the door and freedom. As they crossed the foyer, McKinnon took a newspaper from the rack and tucked it under his arm, then escorted her into the elevator.Once in his room, McKinnon spread the newspaper open to the Entertainment section, and she or he concept, my God, he is going to take me to a rattling film!"What appears accurate to you, Charly?" He became searching at the page as he asked the question. The bed is the handiest thing that pastimes me, McKinnon, she concept and once more skilled the acquainted feelings as he swung his head up and seemed into her eyes."Humor me, Charly. Have you seen any of those movies before?" She pressured herself to appear far from him, and down at the newspaper. There had been numerous she had visible, however only one she had honestly enjoyed, so she advised him."Good. I've seen it too. That's all I needed to realize." Rolling the paper cup, he jammed it into the wastebasket and kicked off his footwear. "Get snug, Little Witch. The relaxation of this nighttime is ours. If everybody asks the next day, which they might not, that's the film we noticed." His tie and match coat were flung carelessly over the lower back of the nearest chair, and he unbuttoned the pinnacle three buttons of his blouse. Again, she had the feeling of having performed this scene once more.Before she knew what turned into happening, he had picked her up, eliminated her footwear, and plan, and led her gently to the bed. Stretching out beside her, one arm below his head, one knee barely raised, he looked up at her. "Beats the little SUV or the Caddy, huh, Witch?"Charly was silwasup to now, questioning how he become going to proceed. She smiled at him now, trusting him absolutely and loving him with all of her beings. She settled towards him, then glanced up and requested, "Want to play a few Battleships?"I assume you're joking. There's the handiest one issue I need to do and it is the same component I desired to do the night time we had been stranded together, and each night time because. I do not know the way it happened, Charly, when I swore I could in no way again be at risk of a female, however, I'm in love with you. More in love with you than I ever notion it feasible to be in love." He became twisting a coil of her hair around his finger, and she or he realized that his hand becomes shaking."McKinnon, are you nervous?" Her emotions were so robust and so proper that she had no greater doubts about their destiny. She knew it'd work out in a few styles that changed into high-quality for both of them, and he or she turned into content material to permit it to take place.Rolling away from her, McKinnon slid off the bed and went to the table to pour them each a glass of wine. She had discovered that the administrators all saved liquids available in their rooms, even though a number of them didn't drink. She knew McKinnon rarely drank because they had mentioned it the nighttime they have been out to dinner collectively.Handing her the glass, he sat beside her on the bed and took a sip of wine. Setting the glass down, he unbuttoned his shirtsleeves and rolled them as much as his elbows as although he located them limiting. He ran his hand through his hair, inflicting it to stand up on one side, then tried to flatten it down again. She found out he was extremely frightened about something, but couldn't believe that the chance of creating love along with her will be the cause."Bear with me, Charly. This is hard for me. It's so long on account that I've truly communicated with everybody that I'm a piece rusty." He took every other sip of wine, then set the glass aside and swung his legs up onto the bed beside her. He pulled the pillows up in the back of their heads and located an arm around her shoulders. Then he shifted his position again and fussed with the pillows yet again."For Pete's sake, McKinnon, relax and communicate! I won't chew. I might even assist you if hit a tough spot. Just talk to me, due to the fact your anxiety is starting to rub off and I become feeling tremendous."Taking a deep breath, McKinnon began to speak, softly before everything, then with more electricity and conviction. "When I went to Australia, Charly, I became going for walks for my existence. All the matters about clearing out 'garbage' were happening to me and I wasn't positive I ought to cope with it without help. But most of it had to do with my ex-wife and my feelings approximately what had come about between us. I simply didn't need to contain you in that. But you have been proper. I do experience an awful lot lighter inner when you consider that I bumped off all those terrible feelings. And for that I thank you." He paused to accumulate his mind and he or she waited quietly, not involved in his restlessness and tension. He became doing just exceptional on his personal."After I was given to Australia and my recollect of goals dried up, I felt deserted and a bit misplaced and I picked up the cellphone a dozen times to call you. But I resisted because I nonetheless had numerous stuff to cope with. I spent maximum of the holiday wandering around on my own and I'm positive my spouse and children think I'm more than a chunk extraordinary."That is going with the turf, McKinnon. Quite a few people have considered me ordinary, over the years, however it hasn't hurt me any. Go beforehand."Well, I finally needed to admit to myself the truth - the truth that I am in love with you. Studying your dreams, reading the interpretations, waiting impatiently for your notes - all of these things need to have advised me, however they didn't. It wasn't till I was roaming around on the opposite facet of the planet that I sooner or later realized what I had to do."Picking up her left hand, he carried it to his lips, urgent them firmly against her grandmother's ring. "Will you permit me to update this with my mother's ring, Charly? Will you marry me?" He spoke the words as though they were pressured out of him earlier than he was geared up. "I sense like the little youngster in ninth grade asking his math instructor for a date, however, this is not a crush. I love you, Charly."Turning to him, she placed her arms around him and held him towards her, giving him reassurance, warmth, and, love. Kissing him briefly, she slid her grandmother's ring off and set it on the night desk."I'm all yours, McKinnon. I assume I became from that first moment you barked at me within the boardroom. I simply in no way allowed myself to hope that we might be married, due to the fact I knew how deeply your spouse's moves hurt you. I had hoped the desires would assist you to get to clearing off all the negatives, however, I'm, amazed at how quickly you've achieved it. You get an A+."Pulling her down greater intently to him, McKinnon heaved a sigh of alleviation. "I'm happy it is settled. Now, will you please shut up? You continually did talk too much." His lips closed over hers and this time they lingered, straying to her eyes, her nostril, her ears, as he showed her with his body how tons he cherished her along with his heart.In closing Charly became capable of delivering him all of her love, in each manner she had ever imagined, understanding that the course they had been on could beautify the feelings they had for every different, as they found out extra about themselves and have become more entire, each as people and as a pair. She had so much extra to educate him - things he was completely blind to, and things that would change him even greater. Her thoughts pulled back to the things McKinnon became doing to her and she gave herself up freely to his lovemaking, becoming a member of him with ardor, love, and popularity in their union.

"Hi, Little Witch. Did you sleep nicely?" McKinnon became smiling down at her, his head propped up on one hand. Charly blinked, stretched, then smiled lower back at him, pulling his head down for a very good morning kiss. He slid lower back beneath the covers and accrued her near him again, groaning as he glanced at his watch. "Charly, we ought to be on the Prayer Breakfast in twenty-five mins, searching respectable, presentable, and as although we'd simply spent the evening at a movie after which went to bed early."Well, McKinnon, you acquire a part of it right, anyway." Charly chuckled at him. "What takes place if we simply spend the rest of the day proper here? Do we get hung at sunrise?"No, but we've got each director leering knowingly at us for the relaxation of the convention and I do not need that for you." He yanked the covers off of her and gave her a bit push in the direction of the edge of the mattress. "Quick, into the bathe, and I'll help you wash."Hopping out of bed, Charly appeared to return to him. "I concept you stated we needed to hurry, McKinnon." She became turning the water on inside the bathe while the cellphone rang, so she didn't pay attention to the verbal exchange that was served.McKinnon grabbed it before the second one ring. It becomes the supervisor. "Have you seen Charly, T. G.? Nobody appears to recognize wherein she is and we're getting a piece involved." He sounded flustered and McKinnon questioned what the hassle was, so he requested. "What's the problem? wanted toed to allow recognize to recognize lecture is canceled, so she will be able to sleep in if she desires to, however,r she's not answering her telephone."McKinnon paused, and the burned his bridges. "It's okay, John. I'll see that she gets the message."There changed into an extended silence, then a low whistle. "Well, McKinnon, you've got my blessings. Take the morning off and I'll make your excuses for you. My, my, my." And he hung up. Stepping into the shower, McKinnon took the soap from Charly. "If you can have one desire right now, Little Witch, what would it not be?" He started out soaping her lower back, sliding his arms around her body in near hers. She moved towards him, playing with the warmth of the water as it cascaded over them. "Just if you want to live here with you for the relaxation of the day." Reaching up, she pulled his head down for a long, gradual kiss."Granted. You see, I too, have my unique powers."Charly pulled lower back and seemed up at him. By the grin on his face, she knew he became telling the reality. As he defined what had taken place, she blushed, then remembered that in only a brief time they could be married, so she gave herself as much as the joy of loving him and being cherished, stable inside the know-how that they might conquer any challenges they may meet in the destiny. And so it changed into that the goals became fact and truth became a dream.